Ben and Arald

and The Lost Baby

written and illustrated by

Karel Henneberger

Published by
THE KEMSH PRESS

-USA-

WriterKMH@gmail.com
A KEMSH Company

First Printing

LIBRARY OF CONGRESS CATALOGING-IN-PUBLICATION DATA

Henneberger, Karel, 2019—
Ben and Arald and The Lost Baby/Karel Henneberger

ISBN 978-1-5323-4636-1

Printed in the United States of America
Printing Impressions, Martinsburg, WV

Dedicated to:

Al, always my best friend

And Benjamin who inspired the original story

With Thanks to:

The Writers of the Desert Rose Café
And the Squid Squad of Waynesboro YMCA

KEMSH

2019

"Dragons are more important to this world than almost anyone could know." Merlin in *Harry Potter and the Children of the Clan* by Swissdog, 2012

"Dragons possess great power and wisdom."
Kuan in *Tail of the Dragon* by Bonnie di Marco, 2018

History and Science in Ben and Arald stories:

The Hidden Valley holds mysteries that are found only in Ben and Arald stories. But many true things are just as strange. There really is a green volcanic rock called Acasta Gneiss (Ah-cast-ah Nice). It is billions of years old and is only found near Hudson Bay in Canada—except for Qua-nya-tse-né (Kwa-nyah-say-nay), the *Great Green Rock of God* in Hidden Valley.

Every day we learn new facts about our world. What we call magic may simply be something we don't understand yet.

Scientists explore the world to discover how things work. Historians explore records to learn what happened in the past. Both kinds of explorers are missing pieces of the real puzzle. More exploration is needed.

Ben and Arald have experienced a few of those missing pieces. Someday, maybe scientists and historians will find them, too.

More **History and Science in Ben and Arald stories:**

Spanish sailors put rocks in the bottom of their ships as ballast to help keep them upright during storms. Many Spanish ships sank just off the Colombian shore in the 1500s. Earthquakes and big waves may well have pushed an unusual rock to the shore.

The Koqui Indians really do live on a pyramid-shaped mountain in the north of Colombia, South America. They believe that they have been placed there by the Creator to keep the world in balance. The other Colombian natives seldom meet with the Koqui, but an unusual stone would have been taken to them as a gift.

Quetzal Children are small dragons, children of Quetzalcoatl, Aztec god of light, justice, mercy and wind. He is usually pictured as a feathered serpent.

The Big Empty: Scientists know that there are parts of 'empty' space where there is nothing that we can see. Scientists all over the world are very excited and are working hard to learn exactly what is there. The Great Dragons are looking into it, too.

List of Characters

[aka = also known as]

United States:

Ann (Andrews) Drake: Ben's mother

Arald: North American dragon. Son of Tahli. Dragon-bound to
Benjamin

Benjamin Thomas Drake aka Benmin, Pennamin: 13-years-old.
Dragon-bound to Arald

Bracken and **Gorse**: mules that come when needed

Grammy Andrews: Ann's mother

Hidden Valley: an area with a still-open portal to the Dragon
World

James Drake: Ben's father

Jeanie Drake: Ben's 17-year-old sister

Oma aka Azzie: James Drake's sort-of grandmother. Dragon-
bound to Tahli

Polter: North American dragon. Dragon-bound to Kembe (see
Dragon World characters).

Qua-nya-tse-né (Kwa-nyah-say-nay): the guardian rock in the
center of Hidden Valley

Tahli: North American dragon. Mother of Arald. Dragon-bound
to Oma

Colombia, South America:

Bruyah aka Pru'ah: Kocqui Mamos-to-be.

Ha-guy: Kocqui guide

Kisin: Kocqui Mamos (Chief). Dragon-bound to Yochi

Nah'ee: The Lost Baby

Señor Bogado aka Myku: a Kocqui tribe member who works between the outside world and the Kocqui tribe.

Señora Maria: Señor Bogado's wife

Yochi: South American dragon. Dragon-bound to Kisin.

Dragon World:

Arose, Chobah, Taranoka, and **Penmose**: Great Dragons

Eldest Great Dragon: mother of Nah'ee, the Lost Baby

Kembe aka The Old Man, Gem'bah: Oma's sort-of grandfather. Dragon-bound to Polter

Polter: North American dragon. Dragon-bound to Kembe. Went to Colombia with Oma and Ben.

Arald   Tahli   Polter

Chapter One—Polter

"Be quiet, Arald," I grumbled sleepily. I pulled the edge of my pillow over my head. The first day of summer vacation and Arald had to wake me up before dawn!

"*Am quiet*," Arald said. Well, he didn't exactly *say* the words. Dragons don't really talk in words. Most people hear a kind of chirping or chittering or something. But I've been dragon-bound to Arald since he hatched last summer. I 'hear' a combination of pictures and colors in my head and get what he means.

I groaned again. A claw pulled at my pillow. "*We all talk quiet together.*"

"Unngh." I grabbed hold of the pillow corner. Usually, being a dragon partner is fun, but there are times...I slowly lifted one eyelid and a dragon's eye swirling with dark reds and blues looked back. NOT Arald.

Ben and Arald and The Lost Baby

Karel Henneberger

"Too young. Not think enough. Will not do." The sharp colors of his voice made me wince and there were more smells than pictures as he shouted inside my brain.

I sat up. Fast. "Arald?" I looked around. Two dragons. I blinked. No. THREE dragons. Arald with his red and gold fur fluffed out with excitement, the mean one, and... Tahli.

"Tahli! Is Oma okay? What happened?" I *never* see Tahli without Oma. I swung my feet off the bed and reached for yesterday's shirt on the floor.

"Azzie well," Tahli told me silently. *"She comes. I bring Polter."*

"Polter?" I looked at Arald while I tried to jam one foot into a shoe. Wrong shoe. I fished under the bed with my other foot.

Arald nodded. *"Polter. Dragon-bound to Old Man."*

I sat still, my toes gripping the sock stuffed inside the shoe, one arm partly in the shirt sleeve. Oma's Old Man? The mean dragon was sitting on the bed rail—sort of. Dragons can be invisible when they want or need to. Oma calls it 'going neutral.' I could still see the dresser behind the old dragon, so he hadn't gone entirely neutral. "Polter?" Tahli and Arald nodded, bowing slightly toward the old dragon. He wasn't much bigger than Arald. Polter's skin showed through his brown-gold fur in spots and his eyelids drooped. He kind of hunched down a bit, too. Well, if he was partner to the Old Man, then he'd be really, really old.

It seems that dragon-bound folks live a long time. A very long time. Most people think Oma is Dad's grandmother, but I learned last summer that she's a whole lot more than that! In the first place, she was dragon-bound to Tahli, a North American dragon, back during the War. The *Civil* War. 1864. That war. And the Old Man was a couple of *centuries* older than Oma. He was her several greats-grandfather. The Old Man and his dragon partner, Polter, went off to explore the Big Empty more than a hundred years ago and never returned. Or maybe they had.

Dad peered around the bedroom door. "Good. You're awake." He came in, pushed aside some dirty clothes, and stepped around a pile of history books. I do love history, especially since I learned how long dragon-bound humans live. He nodded at Arald, then, "Ah. Tahli. You're looking well."

I jumped up, stumbling a bit with one foot still caught in that shoe. "Dad! Oma's coming! And the Old Man came back."

"So Tahli has already told you," Dad said. "Good. Better get packed. We'll head for the airport right after breakfast."

"Huh?" I shook my head. "Pack? Tahli said Oma's coming here and Polter said..." I made a face and rolled my eyes, "he said that Arald and I do not think enough and we're too young. But he didn't say too young for what."

"Polter?" Dad asked. Tahli chirped a short phrase and Polter looked a bit more solid.

"It's hard for him to show himself," I explained. "He's really, really old, you know." The old dragon's eyes began whirling again. I grinned. One point to me.

Dad frowned. "Benjamin Thomas Drake!"

I sighed. Polter had deserved that, but..."Sorry, Polter," I mumbled. I sat back on my bed, finished putting on my shirt, and sighed again. "Pack for what, Dad?"

"Oh. Of course. Oma's meeting us at the airport. All of you are needed in Colombia. It's a dragon thing."

"Columbia? Why the airport? South Carolina's not far."

"No. Co*lom*bia—South America."

"Baby Dragon lost. Great Dragons say we go." That was Arald. He tipped his head up twice—yes, yes. *"We go. Benmin-Arald. Oma-Tahli. Polter."*

"Something to do with the Great Dragons," Dad said at the same time, "and you know—What Dragons decree..."

"...shall certainly be," I said, with a frown, finishing the phrase Oma uses whenever I question the reason for doing something that doesn't seem to make sense. I looked over at Tahli, but she and Polter had either left or gone neutral all the way.

"Left," Arald said, answering my thought. He fluffed his fur a bit. *"Great Dragon baby. Portal too small. Mama is..."* Arald blinked and tilted his head for a second the way he does when he's 'talking' to Tahli. His eyes grew big and started swirling green with surprise. *"Mama is Eldest Great Dragon!"*

The Eldest Great Dragon! Arald and I had to go into the Dragon World last year and we met the Eldest Great Dragon. A bit scary. Well, a lot scary. "She hasn't been in this world for...well, since forever," I said.

"Not *quite* true." Dad frowned. "But most portals between the two worlds have been nearly closed for a thousand years.

Great Dragons are the big ones. The ones we read about in stories. It isn't true that they had always destroyed things and ate people for fun. Most of the dragons in the Dragon World *are* definitely anti-human—for some really good reasons. Seems some Great Dragons were stuck in this world when the portals got too small. Then humans hunted them to extinction. That doesn't make many friends. And before that, people stole dragon eggs to use in trying to make gold or to prove how brave they were or something equally stupid. And dragons have *very* long memories.

But some dragons still live in our world. Small dragons like Arald and Tahli. And Polter, though he hadn't been in this world for many years. Their wingspans are only about two or three feet from tip to tip. Great Dragons have *claws* that big.

I stared at Dad. He stared back at me. "So," I said slowly. We're going to Co*lom*bia to find a baby Great Dragon. A baby dragon from an egg the Eldest Great Dragon laid over a thousand years ago."

Arald jerked his head upwards. *"Yes."*

"But how did it get to Colombia," Dad asked, frowning. "The Great Dragons were in Europe and Asia, mostly. Some in Africa, but not the New World."

We both looked at Arald. He cocked his head again. Then he shrugged. Tahli and Oma didn't know, either.

Dad leaned his hands on his knees and stood up. "We'll talk more at breakfast. Now get dressed and think about what to take with you. Chop-chop."

Arald

Chapter Two—A Secret Uncovered

At the bottom of the stairs, I sniffed. Mom's oat flour pancakes. Yum. Arald sat on my shoulder as usual. He fluffed out his wings a bit, hitting my ear. *"Sit still or they'll know you're here,"* I said silently.

He dipped his head. *"Sorry. Need honey. Energy for trip?"* I heard inside my head.

"You'll make a mess," I thought back to him, "but okay. Honey on pancake pieces."

He ducked his head and twisted to look at my face. *"Need bacon, too?"* he said slyly, his eyes open wide.

Ben and Arald and The Lost Baby   Karel Henneberger

I shook my head and smiled. "Bacon, too," I added as I moved toward the kitchen door. We had the routine down pat. Arald goes neutral until I'm at the table. Luckily, Mom started using long tablecloths about the time Arald and I came back from Oma's at Christmas. Arald has to be visible to eat, but he sits by my feet and I slip him what I can. He especially likes thick-sliced bacon.

We were almost at the kitchen door when I heard Mom say something that made me slam on the brakes.

"He has to know, Jim. We have to tell him *now*."

"I thought we'd have time to ease into this," Dad said in a kind of sad voice. "But you're right. He has to know." He sighed.

I slapped the door open. "I have to know *what?*" I demanded, suddenly angry. I *don't* like secrets. Well, people keeping secrets from *me*, anyway.

Mom looked at me, then at my shoulder. "Well, nice to see you at last, Arald."

I think my heart stopped beating. I know I stopped breathing. Mom wasn't supposed to know about dragons. Only Dad and Oma. My eyes slid to where Arald was sitting on my shoulder. He should have gone neutral. He hadn't. He sat there, claws folded in, wings tucked neatly, and his crest proudly raised.

"U-uh. Y-you know!?" I stuttered.

"We intended to tell you this weekend while Jeanie is off with Grammy shopping for college stuff. We couldn't tell you before because you had to prove you can keep such a huge secret."

Mom knows. Mom knows about dragons. The thought swirled around in my head, making me dizzy. I looked at Arald.

He blinked and tilted his head. He was 'talking' to Tahli. *"Oma say yes."*

"Who else?" I almost yelled. "Grammy? Jeanie? *Her* friends?" I *hate* people keeping secrets from me. Especially secrets about dragons. About *my* dragon. Keeping knowledge of dragons secret from others is one thing. Keeping me—*me*, dragon-bound to Arald—in the dark about who also knows is another. An entirely different thing.

"Definitely *not* Grammy or your sister," Dad laid his arm around my shoulder. He gave me a little push toward my chair, but I wasn't about to move until I knew what was going on. "Neither of them could keep a secret if their lives depended on it."

Mom grinned. "My mother is a wonderful woman. She has great people skills and is interested in just about everything. Jeanie is much like her."

I rolled my eyes. "Yeah. Right." Grammy is nice and funny. Jeanie's favorite pastime is telling everyone how stupid I am. "Jeanie is…a pain."

"Ben-ja-min?" Dad said warningly.

"Well, she is," I insisted. "She's always telling her friends about how dumb I am. And she goes through my stuff, too."

"Jeanie and Grammy are both cut from the same cloth," Mom said. "They both are interested in everything, but they just can *not* keep from telling what they know—about anything."

"Which," Dad continued, pushing me a little harder, "is why, while Jeanie is away for a few days, we wanted to tell you." The push became a shove. I plopped down on my chair. Arald gracefully–well almost gracefully—stepped off my shoulder and onto a chair beside me. "But now, with you leaving for Colombia and all…"

Mom looked at me with a worried look. "Ben, I've known about Oma and Tahli since before your Dad and I got married."

"H-how? W-why?" I stammered.

"I couldn't marry someone who wouldn't accept something as important to me as Tahli." Dad put his arm around Mom. "We went to see Oma one day, and…I think she knew I wanted your Mom to know."

"That was the first time I'd met Oma," Mom said. "Somehow I'd pictured her differently. But there she was—as tall as your father and with that copper-pot scrubber hair piled on her head."

"Her hair hardly ever moves, you know," I said, not really paying attention to what I was saying.

Mom nodded. "We had just finished dinner when suddenly," Mom paused, scrunching up her face, "suddenly, there was this *creature* sitting on Oma's chair back. Scared the heck out of me, I'll tell you. That was my first experience with a dragon."

"But she was soon offering Tahli grapes," Dad said proudly.

"And then I was exposed to Oma's animals, her popping in and out, and the house that seemed to change." Mom smiled at Dad, patting his cheek. "And finding out Oma's history. That was amazing. There's a lot I still don't understand, but I believe."

I grinned, remembering when I first saw Tahli with brassy-gold fur and kind of sparkly purplish eyes, as she appeared out of nowhere. "Tahli's really a wyvern, Mom. Wyverns have two wings and two feet. Most of the Great Dragons have two wings and four feet."

"Well, I am certainly glad Oma doesn't have a Great Dragon," Mom said, her eyes wide. "Tahli and Arald are just the right size, I think."

I thought for a minute while I took three pancakes from the serving dish. I concentrated on placing the pancakes just so on my plate. "What would have happened if Mom hadn't believed you?" I asked Dad, not looking at him. I wasn't sure if I really wanted to know the answer.

Dad frowned. "Oma said she wouldn't have remembered. I'm not sure how, but dragons *do* protect their secrets."

Mom smiled. "But I *did* believe—and kept their secret. And I saw how excited you were when you showed the egg to your dad last year. He wasn't sure twelve was old enough to keep such a big secret, but I reminded him that he had been even younger."

She cut up one pancake and drizzled honey on top, then put the plate on the table. "Hop up here, Arald. I'm so happy to finally get to see you. You are quite handsome, you know."

Arald ducked his head and his nose got red like it did when he caught a claw in his wing. He hopped up on the arm of my chair, quickly grabbed a piece of the honeyed pancake with one claw, and neatly nibbled it. His tongue caught a drip of honey before it hit the plate.

"Keeping the secret wasn't so hard for me," Mom said sitting down and pushing the honey closer to me. "I didn't have a dragon to hide. And I was older. Keeping secrets seems to get easier as you age. Maybe because you have more to keep."

"When did you find out, Dad?" I asked, stuffing half a pancake in my mouth.

"I was only six when I went to live with Oma," he said. "That age accepts the unbelievable easily."

I closed my eyes, remembering how I had felt when I held the strangely splottled egg, and how the chickens all bowed their heads when I caried it out of the hen house. Arald nudged my cheek with a slightly sticky nose. I sighed happily and shook my head to clear it. "I saw the plaque at the train station in Hopers Valley and remembered Oma said she helped build it so the train could bring soldiers home. *Civil War* soldiers! That's when I knew she wasn't really your grandmother, Dad."

"Oh, she is…just with a few greats in front," Dad said, a far-away look in his eyes.

"I'm so proud of you, Ben." Mom offered Arald more pancake. Of course, he took it. "He'll soon stop eating so much," Mom said, seeing me frown at him. "He's almost finished growing." She paused. "So you can stop hiding food for him now."

Ben and Arald and The Lost Baby

Karel Henneberger

I ducked my head. So that's why there was always stuff out on the counter. I grinned at her and swallowed the last piece of pancake. "Let's get you cleaned up, grubby face."

"Grubby Face," he admitted cheerfully, a piece of bacon still in his claw. *"Happy belly."*

Dad looked at his watch. "Better get a move on. We have to be at the airport an hour early, you know."

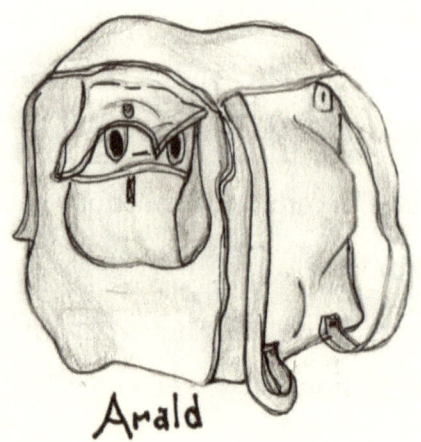

Arald

Chapter Three—Flying

Arald was excited. Well, I was, too, but Arald could hardly remember to stay concealed in my pack. Until late last year, Arald hadn't been able to go completely neutral. He'd kind of fade out like the Cheshire Cat in *Alice in Wonderland,* usually leaving his tail visible.

Last year, I'd cut the back of one pocket out of my pack, leaving the flap so he could peek out and still not be seen. That worked when we went down to Hoper's Valley to sell eggs, but it had not been as good coming home on the train.

I had finally propped my pack up against the window and pushed the pocket flap up so Arald could watch as the world went by. His wriggling still attracted some attention, so I had to wiggle around, too. I have no idea what people thought of me acting like a three-year-old who couldn't sit still.

He was just as bad when we got to the airport. I could feel him squirming around in my pack, trying to see everything. "If you can stay neutral," I told him silently, "you can sit on my shoulder." The words hadn't left my mind before he was trying to crawl out of the pack. "Wait a minute! Let me set the pack down first." I managed to get the pack open just in time. Arald was in neutral, but he was excited and shoved me backwards. I pretended to root in the pack while he got himself under control and seated on my shoulder. That lasted long enough for us to get from the car into the airport proper.

Oma was already there with our tickets. She handed me a passport. "Where did this come from?" I asked her. "It takes weeks to get one." I knew because a friend had almost not gotten hers in time to go to France to visit her grandparents last Christmas.

"What dragons decree…" she said, smiling.

"…shall certainly be," I finished. "They could have made a better picture, though."

Oma just smiled and picked up a bag that looked like it had been made out of some rug. I remembered reading about carpet baggers. After the Civil War, men from the north went south to take advantage of folks who had lost most everything. Their bags were made from carpets, so 'carpet baggers.' I guess Oma didn't travel much and still had the bag left from before people had real suitcases or duffle bags.

Arald had to go back in the pack once we were on the plane. There were too many people around for him to be out. Apparently, the Great Dragons decreed that we get first class attention, so it was just Oma and me in the row—as far as anyone else knew, anyway. I don't know where Tahli was, but nobody screamed, so she might have been sleeping or gone somewhere.

Arald stopped wriggling to check. *"Sleep. Polter, too."*

"Polter's still here?" I asked him.

"Polter come with us," he said, adding, *"Why?"* I shrugged.

The old put-the-pack-by-the-window-so-Arald-could-see-out trick worked for a while. But by the time they served lunch, Arald was really hungry. With him still in my pack, we were able to make do. I put a piece of food on the arm of my seat next to Oma and he extended one claw and slipped the food through the pocket flap. *He* felt better and settled down a bit, but *I* was still hungry.

Ben and Arald and The Lost Baby   Karel Henneberger

We landed in Miami and practically had to run to the other end of the airport to board the plane to Houston, Texas at the last minute. That one was just as big, but not as full of people. No meal, but my snack went into the pack and into Arald's stomach. Anything to keep him quiet and happy. Oma nodded her approval and offered me her snack. "Tahli has stopped growing and so have I," she said with a smile. First class snacks are fine, but they didn't fill *my* stomach.

In Houston, we had to wait over an hour. Tahli popped back in, but almost instantly went neutral, so nobody noticed. There was no place to let the dragons free, so Arald had to stay in my pack. Tahli and Oma mind-talked to Arald some. I could hear them, but since what they said was aimed only at Arald, I could only guess that they were telling him to behave. He grumbled, but calmed down. Polter didn't show at all.

Finally, we boarded another, smaller plane for the trip across the Gulf, into Mexico, and then on to Colombia. The smaller plane had only a few passengers, but lots of boxes of cargo in the open space in the back. I was able to let Arald out to explore the boxes. "Mind you stay away from the people, Arald," I told him sternly. "Don't let them see you."

"Won't see. Only explore. Stretch wings," he assured me.

"Well, don't stretch too much."

"Tahli says, too." He sighed. *"Only want to see. So much new."*

"Well, save some energy for Colombia," I said. I grinned, though. I was almost as excited as he was. I'd never flown in a plane either. At least Arald had flown using his wings. I looked out the window, but there wasn't much to see. Just water, what looked like toy boats, and more water.

I was really getting hungry by then. Mom had packed several breakfast bars and a couple of water bottles in my pack. But Arald had found the bars and all that was left of them were the wrappings. His stomach was full, but mine wasn't.

One of the passengers near the front got up and rummaged in a metal box behind the pilot. He pulled out a half-dozen bags and bottles of water and handed them around. The bags were vacuum packed with pictures of some kind of food on them. I was glad that I'd been able to bring my knife along. Seems Dragon power can keep x-rays from seeing what dragons don't want seen.

I used my pocket knife to slit one open. Hmmm. Rice and some herbs and maybe chicken. Cold, but filling. Then Oma showed me how to simply unzip the top. No matter. My stomach was happier and that was enough for me.

Then we hit some bad weather. Arald came back and crawled into my pack. *"Too bouncy,"* he said. *"Boxes hurt."*

"Well, keep quiet. They don't allow animals on the plane unless they're caged," I warned him.

"Not animal. Am dragon," he told me silently, digging one claw through the canvas and into my back.

"Ouch! I know that and you know that. But other people don't. So just behave! And stop clawing me."

Arald settled down some after that. I think Tahli spoke to him again. I heard him sniff a couple of times. *"You okay, Arald?"* I asked.

"Not sad. Hungry. Mom food gone. Only good smell left."

"Yeah. I noticed," I told him with a smile.

Just then Oma got up, said something to the pilot, and pulled another bag of food from the metal chest. "Can't have a hungry dragon, now can we?" she whispered. I grinned, opened the bag and slipped it into the pack. I had to pretend to chew to cover Arald's noisy eating.

"Good. Better hot, but good."

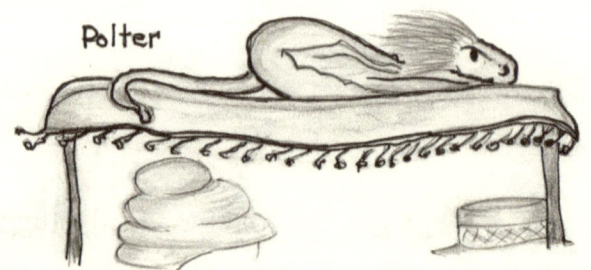

Polter

Chapter Four—Colombia

At the Colombian airport in Medellin, Oma was greeted by a short man with dark eyes that didn't seem to focus on any one thing. "Señor Bogado?" Oma asked, reaching to shake his hand.

The man nodded quickly a couple of times, grabbed her hand and gave it a jerky shake. His head swiveled in all directions as if he was afraid of something—or someone. Maybe he was, because he kept saying, 'dar prisa,' and waving us to hurry. I had to scurry to keep up. I could feel Arald moving in my backpack. I knew his head was peeking out. "Keep neutral, Arald," I thought to him.

"Am. New smells here. Fly?" he asked hopefully.

"NO!" I said in a silent shout. Then a bit more quietly, "We don't know what or who's here. Just wait."

Arald cocked his head and sighed. *"Tahli says no, too."*

"Well, you can watch, but stay neutral," I said out loud. Oma looked back at me, shaking her head. I scrunched my mouth shut. Tahli. She was listening to us.

"Tahli hears not always," Arald voice came slowly, but silently.

"Yeah. But too often," I thought back as I hurried to catch up with Oma and the strange man. I couldn't see him nod, but I could sense it. Kind of like a nudging inside my head.

The man motioned us to hurry and opened the door of a sort of car. Not a regular car with four wheels, doors, and a top. The car did have wheels, but only three. And no sides, no doors, and only a flimsy top with patches and things dangling. It did have seats, but no seatbelts.

Once our bags were tucked behind the seats, we took off with a screech. It must have taken another layer of rubber off those tires. We swerved first one way, then the other, barely missing cars and trucks that were also moving just as wildly. Horns blared and beeped and people shouted words that were probably not polite ones.

The next few minutes were as almost as bad as my first trip with Oma when she was worried about Tahli laying an egg— Arald's egg. She'd been worried it would hatch and nobody would be there to be dragon-bound. If that had happened, Arald would have gone feral and been a danger to everyone and everything around him.

But that hadn't happened. I *was* there to find his egg. We *were* dragon-bound for life. And we had stopped the Big Empty— well, with help from the Great Dragons, Oma and Tahli, my dad and Bekka, a sort of cousin who now knew the secret about dragons, too. Thinking about that helped keep my mind off what was going on.

But reality kept butting in. I was already clinging with both hands to the seat and Arald's claws were digging into my back as we were thrown back and forth as the driver sped through town.

A large truck straddled the road ahead. I was sure we were going to crash. Then suddenly our driver veered off the road, nearly knocking down people who, luckily, dove out of the way. Some fell into store displays. A couple of men knocked over tables at one roadside café when they jumped. Then with a jerk, we were back on the road just inches ahead of the truck.

Our driver speeded up more. The wind made my eyes water so much I couldn't see where we were going. Maybe that was a good thing. Arald and Tahli kept hidden—Arald in my backpack and Tahli in one of Oma's big pockets. "Polter?" I asked Arald.

He hesitated. Talking to Tahli, probably. *"Polter good at neutral. Stay long time,"* he finally said. *"Too old to change back,"* he added smugly. Tahli chittered and Oma frowned at us.

I was breathing hard and clinging as tightly as I could to the seat. Oma just sat there. Oh, she swayed with the car's motion, but her hair never once moved and she didn't even hold onto the seat. Eventually, we were out of the city and there was less traffic. I could breathe again.

Both dragons climbed out to sit on our shoulders, though still in neutral so nobody could see them. Now that we were moving slower, I could see that the cloth roof of the so-called car sagged a bit. "Polter?" I asked silently.

"Yes," Arald answered.

"Chatter not good," came from the roof. I grinned.

Eventually, we started climbing up the side of a big mountain. The road, what there was of it, was rocky. We swayed one way, then another, all the time bouncing up and slamming down. The driver didn't even try to avoid the rocks or ruts. Arald climbed back into my pack and took a nap. I wanted to follow him. It's a good thing I don't get carsick, though it was close a couple of times.

Ben and Arald and The Lost Baby

We must have traveled for five or six hours. Stopping only to fill the gas tank, but not our stomachs. Not a bad thing, though. My stomach didn't really want food right then.

It was dark when we finally stopped. The man grabbed Oma's bag and called back for us to 'dar prisa' again. We hurried. Inside the small house, Oma held her hand out to the woman standing by the open fire. She spoke in Spanish as fast as the man had.

I had barely begun to wonder how Oma knew Spanish, when Arald said, *"Oma explain later."*

She'd better. I had a lot of questions.

We sat at a wooden table and Señora Maria put dishes of some kind of stew in front of us. I dipped my spoon in and took a tiny bite. YUM! Before I knew it, the bowl was empty and Señora Maria had refilled it. Of course, she didn't know that Arald had eaten more than half of it as he was hiding by my feet. "More?" I silently asked him. Before he could answer, Señora Maria had put a big dish of what looked like filled pastry down. She smiled and said something to Oma, then added two more of the pastries to the plate.

"Want those." Arald reached. I grabbed that one and nibbled it, breaking off pieces for Arald. Like the stew, several of the fried pie-like things were gone. Into two bellies.

My eyes were drooping and Señor Bogado showed me where to go to the bathroom, then dipped water from a pail for me to wash in. Oma and I shared the only bed in the house. I was asleep before I had time to ask Oma how she knew Spanish.

Kisin

Chapter Five—Through the Jungle

I heard strange birds making a lot of noise. Then Arald was poking me. *"Hungry."* So was I. In another room, I could hear Oma and Señora Maria chattering away.

Breakfast was another feast of strange, but delicious foods. Then Señor Bogado said 'dar prisa,' I grabbed my pack, and we were out the door. I thanked Señora Maria—in the only Spanish words I knew other than 'hurry'— "Gracias. Mucho Gracias."

She smiled and patted my head—I hate that. It makes me feel like I'm about 4 years old—and closed the door. Senór Bogado led two mules around the side of the house. Heavy blankets took the place of saddles. He helped Oma climb onto the front mule and handed her carpet bag to her. Then he knelt, held my foot and lifted, raising me enough so I could shove my other leg over the smaller mule.

Both mules jerked forward. I grabbed hold of the edge of the blanket. Señor Bogado walked in front of us and the mules followed him up the narrow, barely-there trail. In a few minutes, we passed between a pair of stone pillars and everything changed.

The mules lurched one way, then the other as they scrambled up the suddenly really steep path. The trees had changed, too. They were darker and thicker and a bit scary. I could just see Arald and Tahli as they flew beside us a little bit off the pathway. Polter didn't do any exploring like the others. He just flew straight from tree to tree, resting until the others caught up. Arald kept up a running commentary about the birds and trees and flowers and rocks and bugs and...

Hmmm. Señor Bogado *must* have noticed the dragons. Why didn't he say something or, at least, look scared or surprised? I asked Arald. There was a long pause, which I knew meant he was asking Tahli, who was asking Oma. Yeah. Oma turned to look at the dragons flying just ahead of us.

"Tahli says man knows dragon," Arald told me, holding his neck high with surprise.

"The baby dragon?" I asked silently.

This time Tahli answered. *"No. Male. Not like us. Feathers. Not fur."*

Well, that gave me something to think about for a while. So. There was another dragon on the mountain. A feathered dragon. I kept a lookout for that feathered male dragon, but I didn't see him.

"Not here now." Arald twisted his head, looking back at me while he flew.

"Careful, Arald!" I called out loud. I sucked in a deep breath as he suddenly veered to the right, turning on his side with his wings close to his sides, barely missing a large tree trunk. Whew! Arald slid to a stop on a large branch and hid his head from me. I knew his nose was as red as an apple. Tahli chittered at him. He ducked his head more. No sense in me scolding him. Tahli did a good enough job of that.

Finally, we stopped for a break. Oma handed out some kind of orangey-green chips Señora Maria had wrapped in a cloth. We sat on logs to eat and drink water from a stream.

"Oma?" I asked, biting on one of the chips. Not bad, but hard to chew. "How come you can speak Spanish?"

Ben and Arald and The Lost Baby

Oma looked directly at me. I swallowed. I knew that look. I was about to find out something she maybe had to think about because it was so long ago.

"Let's see…" she started counting on her fingers. "It was around 1900, I think. My son, Thomas, brought a Cuban wife home from some war or other. I learned Spanish from her." She smiled. "But that was Cuban Spanish, not Colombian Spanish. There are some differences." Oma turned back to Señor Bogado.

Well, that wasn't too bad. I knew Oma didn't like reminding me how old she really was. She'd partnered Tahli near the end of the Civil War—our Civil War—the one in the 1860s—when she was 15 years old. Hmmm. Oma had a grown son when Teddy Roosevelt went up San Juan Hill in Cuba. "So he was Dad's two-greats-grandfather?" I asked. It was kind of fun working out generations from Oma.

"No," Oma said, slipping the packet of orangey-green chips into her pocket. "Thomas and Anna Maria never had children. You are descended from Benjamin, my first son."

She said something to Señor Bogado. Then she turned to me. "Listen and learn, Benjamin. Bogado is the name he is known to the Little Brothers in the valley. Up here, he is Myku. He will tell us why he brings us up this mountain."

Ben and Arald and The Lost Baby Karel Henneberger

While I chewed on the chips, Myku spoke in Colombian Spanish and Oma translated with help from Tahli and Arald. Myku said he was of the Kocqui Indian tribe that live on a pyramid-shaped mountain—this mountain—in the Sierra Nevada range of northern Colombia.

The Kocqui people believe that their mountain is at the center of the world. They are guardians charged by the Creator with keeping harmony in the universe. Myku married outside the tribe and serves as go-between for the Kocqui and the rest of the world. That charge grows harder, Myku told us, as fewer Little Brothers learn the lessons the Kocqui teach.

"So why are we going to the Kocqui?" I asked, rubbing at the back of my neck. It felt kind of tingly. Bug bite, probably. There certainly were all kinds of bugs flying around making a constant buzzing. But the tingle seemed to come from all around, not just from the bugs I could see.

Oma hadn't been able to tell me yet why we had to make this trip. We couldn't talk on the plane and this was the first chance since we got here.

"Lost Baby here," Arald chittered to me at the same time Tahli said, *"Baby of Eldest Great Dragon on mountain."* Oma nodded.

Wow. How did a dragon egg get on a mountain at the center of the world? Tahli answered my unspoken question. *"Eldest Great Dragon not know how egg is here. Egg laid on mountain across big water place."*

Oma turned and smiled. "She means across the Atlantic Ocean. Maybe in what is now Greece or Africa or maybe Spain." Dragons aren't very good at geography. At least not this world's geography.

"Benmin?" Arald looked around. *"Dragon near."*

The Baby?" I asked silently.

"No. Different." Arald said, twisting his neck, trying to find the other dragon.

"Male. Short man knows." Tahli chirped agreement. She felt the presence of another dragon, too. Oma and I looked at each other.

"Feral?" I asked with a little shiver.

"Not feral," Oma said. "Dragon-bound to a human."

I breathed out a long sign of relief. Not feral. That was good. But who was this male dragon-bound to, I wondered?

Back on the trail, Myku led us up an even steeper section of the mountain. We made a sharp right turn onto an even narrower path. Not long after that, we turned into what looked like plain jungle. I squinted and could just see what might pass for the track a squirrel would make. Myku paused. Suddenly, there was an old man in white pants and tunic standing there with a long staff held crosswise, barring the trail…what there was of it.

Chapter Six: The Kocqui

"Arald! Go neutral!" I told him. Tahli already had and there was no sign of Polter. Arald had been flying in the tree tops. I didn't think the man had seen him.

"Tahli tell, too," he said, appearing—or rather not appearing—on my shoulder.

Myku stepped forward and bowed. He spoke in a strange language—not Spanish or English. Something that reminded me of that movie we'd seen in school about the Aztec peoples.

"Short man tells old one who we are," Tahli said silently. She sat in neutral on Oma's shoulder.

The men each gave the other a small bag of something, then talked back and forth a bit. Oma slipped from her mule and helped me down. Just in time, too. Myku turned and led the mules back down the mountain without even saying goodbye.

The old man stalked forward, stopping in front of Oma. He bowed low, then stood back up, held his staff upright and stared into Oma's eyes long enough to make me squirm. Oma stood tall and looked back at him.

"I am Kisin. You are Ancient Mother," he said. His mouth didn't shape the sounds that came out. He touched a carved shell pendant that hung from his neck.

Ancient Mother? Well, that certainly does describe Oma, I thought. But how did this man know that? And how did I understand him?

"Tahli says our words," Arald told me silently. *"You hear what Tahli says."*

Hmmm. Yes. If I concentrated, I could hear both the man's voice and Tahli's words at the same time.

The man—Kisin—led us up the trail he'd barred before. I kept thinking how Oma was someone worth bowing to. Of course, *I* know she's special. She's dragon-bound to Tahli and she's lived a long time. But how did this man know?

Ben and Arald and The Lost Baby   Karel Henneberger

I rubbed the back of my neck again. Not a tingle this time. More like I'd slept on it wrong. I kept plodding along the trail behind Oma.

"Am hungry?" Arald said in a puzzled tone.

"You can't be hungry. You have been eating fruit all the way up the mountain," I thought back to him. Then I realized I was hungry, too. And I shouldn't be, either. Those orangey chips were filling.

More steep trail. More twists and turns. After another hour or so, we turned a corner and there was a small village directly in front of us. A crowd of people pushed back to let us through.

"You have been called to help us rebalance the world," Kisin said, bowing low to Oma.

Oma bent her head in a small bow. "We have been called to help a mother find her lost baby," Oma said, emphasizing 'we' slightly and putting her hand on my shoulder.

The Kisin looked a bit puzzled, but waved us toward the largest house. People appeared from everywhere. Inside, we were invited to sit on cushions placed on woven palm leaf mats.

The old man bowed his head to Oma. "I am Mamos of this village. Please, sit and share our meal." Several women entered, carrying trays of good-smelling foods.

"Uh, Oma?" Arald was digging into my other shoulder with his claws. He had stayed neutral longer than he had ever done before. He couldn't hold it much longer. And he was hungry.

"We have not come alone," Oma told Kisin, nodding at me.

"Okay," I told Arald. With a small pop! he became visible, falling from my shoulder onto the mat. Tahli followed much more sedately. A loud gasp came from the people surrounding us. "Quetzal Children!" "The stories are true!" Some people jerked away, but Kisin and the girl who now sat beside him leaned forward, their eyes wide with surprise—or maybe fear?

I slipped to the mat to help Arald untangle a claw that had gotten hooked in one wingtip. He ducked his head. *"Sorry."*

"No sorry," I thought to him, stroking his back. "Be proud. You stayed neutral ever so long." He stood a bit taller, fluffing his wings. That made people gasp again.

Oma looked directly at Kisin. "These dragons—these Quetzal Children—are our partners. They will help us find the source of the Terror that fills your forest."

I saw Kisin's throat move as he gulped. "For more than..."
he tipped his head up, thinking, "forty generations, only Kocqui
Mamos and a few Chosen have seen Quetzal Children." He
bowed again. This time to Arald and Tahli.

Kisin closed his eyes and drew in a long breath. That's
when I noticed the padding on the shoulder of his tunic. Just like
the padding on my shirt that kept Arald's claws from poking into
my shoulder. I turned to Oma. She raised her left eyebrow and
nodded.

The girl beside him pulled on Kisin's sleeve. She leaned
closer to the old man. "They have no feathers, Mamos," she said
in an almost whisper.

Oma smiled. "These are North American dragons. They
are furred. Great Dragons have scales, other dragons have feathers
or just skin."

"Great Dragons?" Kisin asked, raising one eyebrow—a
skill not everyone has. Dad and I and Oma can do it, but I didn't
know anyone else who could. Maybe it was a 'dragony' thing.

Oma explained about the Dragon World and the portals.
"There is a portal near here, but it is too small now for any but the
smallest dragon to pass through." She paused. "Somehow, a Great

Dragon egg has hatched here, but without her mother, she is lost and afraid. We have been called to bring them together."

The only portal I knew of was the one in Hidden Valley where Oma lived. Dragons protect the Valley from most humans. Satellites can't even see it, so it isn't on any maps. Even the people who live in Hoper's Valley at the bottom of Oma's mountain don't know about it. That portal had still been big enough for Oma to go through when she was younger, but now it was too small for her. I could still make it through—if I really had to. Not something I would look forward to, though. I probably wouldn't fit, either, in a few years. I was already bigger than I had been last summer when Arald and Tahli and I had gone to the Dragon World. The Colombian portal was apparently much smaller than the one in Hidden Valley. Even a baby Great Dragon had to be pretty big. Tahli chirped her 'pay attention' chirp.

"This portal is where?" Kisin asked Oma. "I know of no place as you describe."

"The portal can't be seen by humans," Oma told him. "But there is one and the Baby is too big to fit through."

The Sacred Stone

Chapter Seven—The Sacred Stone

Kisin looked at Oma, then at Tahli and Arald. He nodded, his thumb sliding over the edge of one ear. "The Sacred Stone was an egg?" He looked a bit sick. "We did not know. We failed our duty and the Terror is our punishment."

Oma touched his arm. "You could not know. The Mamos protected the egg for centuries. You did not fail. The Baby's fear causes the Terror and we were sent to help take her home."

Kisin drew in a long breath, then let it out in a shaky sigh. He looked at the girl beside him and drew his chin down sharply. "Bruyah here will recite the history."

The girl licked her lips and stood. She pulled back her shoulders and lifted her chin. The villagers became silent. No sound at all. Arald and Tahli sat back on their haunches, giving all their attention to the girl. "I will tell you the shortest way of how this came to be," Bruyah said in a voice that carried even to those outside the house. She paced the small open area, speaking in cadence with her steps, her fingers moving on a string with knots at irregular intervals.

> "First Mother was the Sea.
> Memory and future.
> Our world was in balance.
>
> Chaos entered the world.
> Men came in monster ships.
> The world needed balance.
>
> Sea worms ate their ship wood.
> Earth moved, waking the Sea,
> Bringing ship wood to land.
>
> The Sea brought ship stones, too.
> Little Brothers brought us
> A Stone warm to the touch.
>
> Mamos named it Sacred.
> The World must be balanced
> So we guard and protect.

Bruyah stopped, looked at Oma, bowed, and added, "Or we did." She sat down, drawing a huge sigh of relief. The audience folded their hands and bowed slightly to her, though some of the older ones frowned as they bowed. Whispers went around the group.

Kisin stood, tapped his staff on the ground twice. People stopped talking. They sat as still as they had when Bruyah had given her speech. "Two hands of nights ago, the Sky grew angry," Kisin said, "and winds tore at the Sacred Stone's house. Bruyah and I worked through the night, making sure the roof held." He sighed and dropped his head to his chest. "When again the Sun came, the Sacred Stone was broken and the Terror was in the forest."

He looked directly at Oma. "That is the end of our knowledge of this," he said quietly. He sat down again.

That must have been a signal, because everyone started talking and reaching for the food. Special trays were placed in front of Oma and me. Arald bounced down and grabbed a piece of fruit. "Arald!" I frowned at him. "Manners!"

"Hungry! Very Hungry!" he mumbled around a mouthful. He swallowed.

Oma laughed. "He is still young and growing fast," she explained to the crowd that had leaned away as soon as Arald had moved. Many smiled.

Kisin offered an especially tasty-looking piece of...something. Arald slowly walked over and using one claw, gently took the piece from Kisin's hand. *"Arald thanks."*

Kisin jerked his hand back. "He spoke to me!" he said. More gasps of surprise. Others had heard Arald, too.

I grinned. "Good job," I told him silently. "I didn't know you could talk to others!"

"Didn't know, either," he said, fluffing his wings and looking proud.

Kisin looked at Oma, his smile changing to a frown. "The Terror grows worse. People have fear. Right now, it comes not, but other times people cannot think beyond The Terror. They cannot sleep. We must find your 'Baby' quickly."

Oma nodded. "Yes, she must be found soon."

Suddenly, that uncomfortable tingly feeling in the back of my head was gone, but another, stronger ache took its place. I looked at Arald. He cocked his head, then shrugged. "Uh, Oma?" I swallowed hard. I paused. "When Arald first hatched, when he was awake, he only thought of food. But he slept most of the time. What if the Terror comes only when the Baby is asleep?"

Oma raised one eyebrow. So did Kisin and Bruyah. Yeah, that has to be something only families with the ability to bond with dragons can do.

Arald jerked his head at the same time that Tahli disappeared. Not gone neutral. Just gone. *"Tahli asks Great Dragons,"* Arald said with awe.

"She went to the Dragon World? From here?" I asked him silently.

He tipped his head down—no. *"Maybe go to portal here? Talk to Great Dragons, not go Dragon World?"*

I grinned. Apparently, the Eldest Great Dragon would do what was needed to get her baby back.

Tahli appeared, but she wasn't alone. Polter, the Old Man's dragon partner popped in beside her. I felt the air splash against me as the two entered the room at the same time. Even Kisin and Bruyah looked shocked when yet another dragon appeared. Surprise and awe rippled through the crowd.

Polter growled to Oma, ignoring the rest of us. *"Must go now,"* he said impatiently.

Tahli chittered. "The Baby is called Nah'ee," Oma told the Kisin and the others. "She is alone and afraid."

Kisin frowned. "In the old language, Nah'ee means 'her dreams are truth.' She is the Terror? Because she fears?"

Oma nodded. She looked around the small room at all the Kocqui. "We must find Nah'ee quickly. What she dreams, happens. As her fears grow so does the Terror."

"So the Baby dragon is named Nah'ee," Bruyah said, leaning forward with a big smile on her face.

I frowned. Why was she so happy? So far, she'd been as grumpy as Polter. It didn't make sense.

"Girl thinks wrong," Arald told me silently.

"What do you mean?" I asked.

"Not sure. Smell wrong? Not understand."

"We must leave now to search for Nah'ee," Kisin said, standing and waving Bruyah to the doorway.

People started moving toward the doorway, staring at the dragons and whispering to each other. "But where to start the search?" Bruyah asked. The world stopped. At least, our part of the world. It was like we were in a game of statues—Oma had one foot in the air, Kisin's hand was raised, everyone was frozen in place, too.

I shook my head. How stupid could we be? Of course, we had to know where to start. Maybe find where the Terror got really, really bad?

Arald tilted his head. Tahli nodded. Polter looked disgusted. *"Portal,"* he said. In a very loud silent voice that made me squint. He stomped in a circle. *"Said before. Not think enough. Too young."* His wings fluffed and fur flew. He leaned forward, hissing. If he could breathe fire, he would, I thought.

"The portal," Oma told the people. "Nah'ee will be trying to get as close to her mother as she can. That would be at the portal."

"You said it was too small to go through," Kisin asked. "You said it couldn't be seen.

"It *is* too small to go through," Oma said, adding, "and it *can't* be seen by people."

"People can't see it," I said, butting in. "But dragons *can*." I nodded at Arald and Tahli. I didn't look at Polter. The portal. Of course. The Eldest Great Dragon had known when her baby hatched. She must have heard it through the portal. It was too small now for anyone to enter, but...

The three dragons disappeared. Arald and Tahli popped back in. The air they pushed out of the way slapped against us just a bit. "Where's Polter?" I asked, standing up straight.

"Old. Can't pop twice," Arald chittered with a wide dragon grin. He didn't like Polter, either. *"He waits ahead. We lead to portal."*

"Our dragons will lead us to the portal," Oma told the others. "We must leave soon. Nah'ee sleeps now. And when she sleeps…"

"She will dream," Kisin finished. "And the Terror returns and grows." Oma and I nodded. Yes. The Terror would return and get worse.

Bruyah

Chapter Eight—The Prophecy

"The closer we get to where Nah'ee is, the more we will feel the Terror," Oma said.

Bruyah moved toward the doorway, shoving people out of the way. "Wait!" Kisin shouted. "We must first prepare."

"Follow her," I told Arald silently. He flew over the heads of the crowd, moving faster than Bruyah could. People ducked and squealed. They'd seen dragons for the first time today. They'd seen them disappear and appear suddenly. They'd even heard Arald talk. But they'd never seen a dragon fly.

"She stops," Arald reported.

Ben and Arald and The Lost Baby Karel Henneberger

Kisin caught up with Bruyah at the edge of the village. I wasn't far behind them. He grabbed Bruyah's arm and swung her around to face him. Arald hovered above where Bruyah stood, her chin on her chest and her hands in fists at her sides. Kisin was saying something the girl didn't like hearing.

Arald plopped down on my shoulder. *"Man say girl must learn patience."* He peered around at me. We both grinned. Yeah. We'd heard that, too—umpty-million times—from Oma.

Tahli chittered a scolding as she and Oma caught up.

"It's just that Kisin said the same thing you have told us so many times," I explained to her.

Oma's mouth smiled, but her eyes didn't. "This is more than a teacher scolding his student," Oma said silently to both Arald and me. "Watch what you say," Oma cautioned.

"Man can hear," Tahli said.

"But he can't understand English. Can he?" I asked her just as silently. I looked at Kisin out of the corner of my eye. Arald ducked his head, but kept his eyes slanted that way, too.

"Do not assume, Benjamin." Oma frowned. "From here on," she said quietly, "you must not speak aloud to Arald. His chittering won't be understood, but your words might."

Ben and Arald and The Lost Baby   Karel Henneberger

"Oma says not all is right here." Tahli spoke silently to me—and to Arald. We nodded. Arald had said the same thing—something smelled wrong. And it had to do with Bruyah.

Just then a Kocqui woman tapped Oma on the arm and handed her a bundle. "Food, blankets," she said through Tahli. "Men make trail, protect." Another woman gave me a bundle and helped me put it on over my pack. Oma slung the bundle crosswise over her shoulder. I did the same. The second strap had to go across my pack, so Arald wouldn't be able to rest there while we traveled. Other women were helping the men put on filled packs, leaving their arms free.

Arald watched as we got everything settled. "Sorry, Arald. You'll have to find someplace else to rest," I told him.

"Can rest on shoulder still. See?" He settled on the padded shoulder, tilting a bit forward as the bundle pushed against his tail. *"Or tree,"* he added, lifting off and flying ahead to land on a branch.

Kisin and Bruyah each shouldered a bundle like ours. We started off. Almost as fast as Polter could say that Arald and I were too young, we were in the forest. Two Kocqui men ahead of us chopped a path using machetes longer than my arm. The three dragons fluttered around in the treetops to direct the path-makers to the portal. Oma, Kisin, Bruyah, and I were next. Two more Kocqui men made up the tail of our caravan. They carried some kind of nasty looking weapons that looked kind of like long wooden swords with pointy stones sticking out on one edge. That bothered me—a lot.

"Not hurt us," Arald said, settling a bit wobbily on my shoulder. *"Protect from animals. But animals afraid. Think we be dangerous,"* he added with another dragon grin.

Oh, yeah. That made sense. Suddenly, I felt something in the back of my head. Not like the tingle I'd felt since coming to the mountain. This time it was more like a bomb exploding. I tried to breathe, but could only stand there and shake. Fear. But more than fear. Terror. *The* Terror. Baby was dreaming again.

"We are close," Kisin said in a shaky voice. He pulled Bruyah to her feet and shoved the men with the machetes forward.

"Hope we don't have to get much closer," I whined silently to Arald, holding my head with both hands. It wasn't pain so much as it felt like my head had a lit fuse in it that was about to explode. There was a bunch of bright sparks pop-popping in my brain and a grayness everywhere else.

We started moving again, but a lot more slowly. It was hard to see through the gray cloud that seemed to hang in front of us. I never imagined fear could actually be *seen*. Arald tucked himself into a ball on my shoulder. I could feel him shivering. Or maybe that was me.

Bruyah dropped back to walk by me. She was shaking, too, but she still acted cocky. "Kocqui know of this. *You* are not Kocqui," she said, sneering at me. She gave me a shove and pushed in front of me again. She spoke louder so I would still hear her. "*I* am the one to find Nah'ee. *I* will be bound with Quetzal's Child. We will fix the unbalance of the world. It is said in the Prophecy."

"Prophecy?" I dropped my hands from my head and frowned. Nah'ee couldn't become her partner. She was going to be with her mother in the Dragon World. At least, worrying about what Bruyah meant was making it easier to deal with the Terror. Or maybe the bad nightmare was almost over. My head felt almost normal.

Arald popped his head up. *"Great Dragons-humans friends…maybe. Partners not."* He tilted a bit, then caught his balance. *"Not understand,"* he added silently. Neither did I, but I agreed. Something was wrong.

"The Prophecy says…" Bruyah started almost marching as she spoke in cadence.

"A time of unbalance
The Quetzal's Child appears.
The Child, Mamos-to-be
Learn together to live.
Balance comes to the world."

She looked back over his shoulder and flashed her teeth. "Nah'ee is the Quetzal's Child. I am to be Kocqui Mamos. I will be dragon-bound with Nah'ee. I will be the most important Mamos ever."

"I tell Tahli," Arald said. He flew ahead. I saw Tahli dip toward Oma. Oma turned and glared back at us. *"Oma angry,"* Arald said a bit worriedly when he came back.

Uh-oh. Now what did I do? *"Not to us. Angry to girl,"* Arald said, shaking his head with relief. Even as scared as I was, I smiled at the shimmer of red and gold as his fur shifted this way and that. *"Benmin fur too short,"* Arald chittered, looking innocent.

"We can't all have red and gold fur," I said silently. "I'd look awful funny if I..." Suddenly, I felt a jackhammer slam into my head. The Terror was back. Nah'ee's dream was worse this time. We were getting closer.

Yochi

Chapter Nine—The Terror

Kisin stood with his staff planted firmly in the dirt. His eyes were wide and his knuckles were white where they gripped the staff. He called out, loud enough to be heard above the Terror that seemed to pound through all sounds in the forest. "We must perform an Honor to the First Mother ceremony."

He pulled Bruyah to her feet and handed her his staff. She was shaking, but she stood straight and held the staff in front of her with both hands.

One of the Kocqui men held on to a thick vine for support and said, "But we have no ceremonial house here. We must go back to the village." The others nodded and whispered to each other.

Bruyah stamped the Mamos' staff on the ground. Once. Twice. The others bowed their heads and stopped talking. Kisin called out again. "We must make a circle here and prepare for the ceremony."

Those with machetes began cutting a small circle into the forest. Those with weapons disappeared, returning quickly with arms filled with large, shiny green-blue leaves. They placed the greens on one side of Kisin's staff and went again into the dark greenness. Another trip and a heap of trumpet-shaped yellow flowers was laid on the other side of the staff.

Oma and I tried to stay out of the way. Bruyah just stood there, staring straight ahead, gripping Kisin's staff with both arms held away from her body.

"Polter near. Other dragon near, too. Not Polter," Arald said, fluttering around me. Tahli settled on Oma's shoulder, but Arald was too excited to land.

I heard Tahli tell Oma, *"This male dragon not feral. But different. Polter waits."*

Hmmm. Not feral. That meant he was bound to a human. But he was not like Polter, either. I looked at Kisin's shoulders. His right shoulder—the padded shoulder—was lower than the other. Something heavy? A dragon in neutral?

"Maybe," Arald answered my thought. *"Very near. Can only feel over Terror if very close."*

Just then Kisin lifted his left hand above his other shoulder. A multi-colored dragon appeared. Bigger than Arald. Bigger than

Tahli, too. The Kocqui who were in the clearing dropped to their knees in shock. Kisin waved them back to their work. They obeyed, but they kept darting looks at him and the new dragon.

"Dragon name Yochi," Tahli told us.

"And dragon-bound with Kisin," I added silently.

"Yes." "Yes." Both Tahli and Arald said at once. *"Others new to see him,"* Tahli added.

Well, that explained the shock. They'd never seen *any* dragons and now there were a handful of them—Tahli, Arald, Polter, Yochi, and the Eldest Great Dragon's Baby.

As if he had heard us, Kisin stalked over to Oma, walking proudly with Yochi on his shoulder. We could see Yochi's iridescent feathers showing reds and greens as the light moved across them.

Yochi and Kisin both bowed their heads to Oma. "Ancient Mother," Kisin said, lifting his eyes to Oma's. Since she was at least a full head taller than he was, that wasn't easy with his head still bent. "I, too, share life with a Quetzel Child. This is Yochi."

"Greetings, Yochi," Oma said smiling at the dragon. "I do hope you can help us." She waved toward Tahli who sat on her shoulder and at me and Arald who was settling down on my shoulder. "You know the hatchling we seek?"

Yochi dipped his head. *"The bringer of Terror."*

We all nodded.

Kisin looked startled. "You hear Yochi speak? None others, not even Bruyah hears his voice."

Tahli rubbed Oma's cheek. *"We are dragon-bound,"* she said a bit smugly. *"We can hear other partnered dragons."*

Arald stood tall and puffed out his chest, trying to look as big as the other male. I grinned. "Yochi is older. You're still growing," I told him silently.

Oma looked at Arald and me, raised one eyebrow, then turned back to Kisin and Yochi. "Nah'ee is the hatchling of the Eldest Great Dragon who is no longer in this world. She awaits the return of her baby to the Dragon World. You can help us find her?"

"Yochi knows where Terror lies." Yochi flexed his wings, sending a few feathers flying.

"Where?" "Where?" Arald and Tahli asked rather loudly—at the same time Oma and I almost yelled, "Where?!"

"Not far." Yochi said with a toothy grin. He reminded me of a boy at school—a boy I avoid as much as possible. Polter was mean, but he was old person mean. Like a man at the branch library in town. He thought every kid was a moron. He frowned all the time and talked to us like we were babies. Yochi, like Geoff at school, just thought *everyone* was stupid—except him.

Ben and Arald and The Lost Baby

Karel Henneberger

"First we must complete the ceremony to Honor First Mother." Kisin turned so quickly that Yochi nearly fell off his perch.

Arald gave a snort and Tahli dipped her head. Even Oma smiled a bit. I didn't mean to grin. Honest.

A rough circle had been cleared. Kisin took his staff back from Bruyah and paced around the edge of the circle. He pointed to spots here and there and the men hacked away a few more pieces from the bushes. Finally, Kisin was satisfied.

Two Kocqui men drew a line directly across the circle, then moved halfway around and drew another line, making a cross in the center. One man carried a folding stool and placed it carefully near the cross. He draped a square cloth over it. The other man carried an armful of flowers and placed them by the stool. A few of the large, shiny green-blue leaves were laid on the other side of the stool.

Kisin stood in front of the stool, facing north. He held his staff in front of him, and stared up at the treetops far above us. Bruyah stood on the other side of the center cross. She looked back at me and grinned in a nasty way as she picked up the flowers.

"She thinks she'll soon be dragon-bound with Nah'ee," I thought.

"Won't," Arald said silently, rustling his wings. *"Can't. Girl wrong,"* he said with a jerk of his head.

Just then, Polter flew down from one of the trees. *"Polter balance circle,"* he said smugly. He looked at Oma and Tahli. *"You be paired."* He looked at the Mamos and Yochi. *"You be paired."* He looked at me and Arald. *"Also pair. Too young. Not think enough."* Then he looked at Bruyah. *"Too young. Polter balance here."*

Kisin nodded. He raised his staff and stamped it twice on the ground.

Chapter Ten—The Ceremony

All the men moved to sit cross-legged on the ground—one man in each quadrant, facing away from the center. They folded their arms across their chests.

Kisin turned and waved Oma and me to go closer. "You are Ancient Mother," he stated, bowing to her. "You have Quetzal Child as do I. This one," he said, pointing to me, "is so honored as well. We must together call on First Mother to guide us." He gestured for Oma and Tahli to stand on his left side and Arald and me on his right. "By tradition, women do not participate in ceremonies," Kisin said to Oma. He continued, "But tradition has already been challenged," he gestured toward Bruyah. "And the Quetzal Child named Polter will balance that quadrant of the Circle."

I glanced at Bruyah. She wasn't grinning anymore. She looked like she had been abandoned. I almost felt sorry for her. Apparently, she's the first girl to be trained to be a Mamos, I thought. I remembered the angry looks some of the villagers had given her when she had told the story. Maybe not everyone was happy that traditions were being changed.

Polter flew to Bruyah's shoulder. She didn't have a padded shirt, so his claws dug in. Spots of blood appeared, but she stood still, barely wincing. "Well, she's brave, anyway," I thought to Arald.

"Maybe. No fear. Angry. Must have fear for brave," Arald said, flicking a claw in her direction. Tahli glared at us. So did Polter, of course. Yochi was too busy being important to notice.

"Those on my left," Kisin said, waving his arm to the left, "are those who 'know more.' Those on my right, are those who 'know less.' They are balanced. You," he looked at Oma and Tahli, "are Ancient Mother and older Quetzal's Child. You are 'know more.' The boy and the young Quetzal Child are 'know less.' You are balanced. I and Yochi are balanced with Bruyah and the oldest Child of Quetzal named Polter. I am old and Bruyah is young. Yochi is young. Polter is old. We are balanced. Above is the sky. Below is the earth. All is balanced. We may begin."

Kisin raised his staff. The forest became silent. No bird sounded. No wind moved the leaves. Nothing. I could hear my heart beating. Kisin swung his staff so the other end was down and made four holes in the dirt—one in each quadrant. He held out his hand. Bruyah handed him the flowers, carefully leaning forward so she wouldn't lose her balance with Polter on her shoulder.

Kisin knelt. Gently, he picked out the stamens filled with pollen. He slowly dropped them into one hole. He placed the petals one by one into the second hole. The grey-green leaves were next. In the last hole, Kisin placed the pendant he wore around his neck. He stood and moved to the stool. He lifted the cloth that had covered the stool, sat down, and draped the cloth over his head.

My leg started to prickle. I shifted my weight. *"BE STILL!"* Yochi hissed. I gulped and stood still.

Kisin raised the cloth and looked up at the sky. "First Mother, Aluna, we ask your help," he said in a slow, deep voice. "We seek the Great Quetzal Child." He paused. "She is afraid and her fear brings Terror to your people." He paused again. "Help us find the Great Child of Quetzalcoatl to bring again balance to the world."

Kisin pulled the cloth over his head again and was still. I really wanted to move. Arald nudged my cheek with his nose. *"Baby awake now,"* he said in a silent whisper. He was right. The

Terror had disappeared sometime during the ceremony. And the tingle in the back of my neck had returned.

So the tingle was what I felt when Nah'ee was awake. We'd been close to her while we were walking up the mountain then.

Kisin suddenly stood up straight. All four dragons spread their wings and took off. "First Mother has answered our plea," Kisin stamped his staff on the ground once. Twice. And said loudly. "We must follow the children of Quetzal."

The men jumped up and came to the center of the circle. The four dragons rose to the treetops. Kisin retrieved his pendant and followed them, Oma close behind. Bruyah and I hurried to keep up. The path-makers ran ahead, slashing at vines and branches so we could follow.

I could hear the wind pushing the leaves and small trees away from us. Birds called again. "Arald?" I called silently.

"We find Baby!" he answered, too excited to keep his voice down. Kisin and Oma turned and motioned us all to be quiet. The men slashing at the vines and branches stopped, their eyes wide open. Kisin waved his hand again and they started working again even harder.

In just a few minutes, we came to a small clearing. Kisin dropped to his knees, staring. Yochi was perched on a broken tree branch. He looked stunned. Polter fluttered down tiredly and landed on a log by the trail. Tahli settled on Oma's shoulder at the same time Arald bumped down on mine. *"Great Dragon Baby,"* Arald whispered aloud.

"Great Dragon, indeed," Kisin muttered quietly. "Quetzalcoatl's Child."

The Kocqui men were kneeling, their hands covering their faces. They darted looks at 'little' Nah'ee. She was sitting on her tail, one leg splayed out awkwardly. The claws of the other leg were tearing apart a whole man-high bush and cramming a wad of leaves into her already full mouth. Her wing claws held on to the bush. She was covered with scales that changed colors as she moved.

"Hungry," Arald said silently.

"Yeah," I told him just as silently. "Me, too."

Oma looked at me. "The hunger isn't yours," she said, smiling. "It is Nah'ee. She has only recently hatched and needs to eat often."

Tahli ducked her head and ruffled her fur. Arald's nose grew red. We all remembered how much Arald had eaten when he was that age. How much he still ate.

Nah'ee looked up. She'd seen us. She stood and stretched her neck high. She was much bigger than Yochi. Standing upright, her head was as high as my waist. "Uh-oh," I stepped back. Nah'ee didn't look happy. She took a step forward.

Oma whispered to Kisin. He stood up. "The Child of Quetzalcoatl is hungry," he announced. "She must be fed. Go. Bring food." The men hurried into the forest and soon returned with piles of leaves in their arms.

Nah'ee took a stumbling step toward us. Tahli and Arald began humming. Yochi soon joined them. Polter kind of rumbled. Nah'ee looked confused. She cocked her head to one side. She stopped, strings of soggy gray-green leaves hanging from her mouth. She blinked several times and plopped down just a few feet from Kisin. Nah'ee looked up at him. He bowed to her and offered her some leaves.

Nah'ee blinked, then faster than I could see, the leaves were in her mouth and Kisin was staring at his empty hands. He waved the Kocqui men forward. Kisin took their armfuls of leaves and sent the men out to bring more.

Nah'ee

Chapter Eleven—The Baby is Found

"We've found her," I thought to Arald. "Now how do we get Nah'ee to the Dragon World?"

"Through portal?" Arald thought back. *"Maybe push?"*

"Okay," I answered. "Let's check the portal while Nah'ee's busy eating." Oma looked over at us and nodded. Tahli nodded, too.

Slowly, Arald and I eased our way around the circle. "The portal must be over there," I said to Arald, pointing toward the rocks behind Nah'ee. I didn't see a zig-zag line in the rock like on the cliff at home. But the dragons seemed to know the portal was close by.

Yochi must have told Kisin what we were doing. When the Kocqui men came back with more leaves and flowers, Kisin moved back, holding the food out and drawing Nah'ee away from the rocks and us.

We got to the rocks and I began feeling along them for that sinking feeling that meant I'd found the portal. Polter sat on a log while Tahli and Yochi flew to help us, their heads twisting and looking back and forth along the rocks. Yochi found it first. His head disappeared into a space in the biggest rock. He pulled his head back and triumphantly announced, *"Found it! I go through now."*

But he didn't. His head and neck went through, but the portal was too small for his body to fit. He pulled back and slumped to the ground as dejected as I'd ever seen a dragon.

Polter popped away. "Gone?" I asked Arald.

"Doesn't like here. He goes to alone place," Tahli said out loud.

Tahli poked at the portal spot, too. *"Too small."* She looked at Arald. *"Arald?"*

Arald left my shoulder and tiptoed toward the portal. He flipped one wingtip at the rock and jerked it back. *"Portal not big. But big enough,"* he said, looking back at me. *"I go through?"* he asked silently.

I drew in a huge breath. "You are the only one who can, I guess," I said silently at the same time Tahli said out loud, *"Only Arald can make it through."*

Ben and Arald and The Lost Baby   Karel Henneberger

I sighed again. Arald and I had gone through the Portal to the Dragon World back in Hidden Valley last year. Not an experience I wanted to repeat. Most Great Dragons really, *really* don't like humans. Dragons have long memories—very long memories. Of course, Arald would be fine. He wasn't human. He had to be fine.

I stroked Arald's back and rubbed him behind his crest. "The dragons don't mind you," I told him silently. "It's only people they don't like."

Arald nodded. He smoothed his head against my cheek. *"Not much afraid."* he whispered silently, standing tall and fluffing out his wings. *"Arald talk to Eldest Great Dragon. Tell her we find Nah'ee."* He looked at the portal, then brushed his cheek against mine. *"Benmin be here?"*

"I'll be here, Arald. Always," I promised.

Arald slipped off my shoulder and flew to the portal. With one backward look, he pushed through and was gone.

Just then, Nah'ee came running toward us. I flattened myself against the rocks, but Nah'ee paid no attention to me or Tahli or Yochi. She ran straight into the portal. Well, not *completely* into the portal. Her nose and one foot made it. I grabbed at Nah'ee by the other foot and pulled. Oma dashed over with

Kisin not far behind. The three of us tried pulling Nah'ee back out. Tahli and Yochi hovered right above us.

One last pull and we all tumbled back onto the ground. Nah'ee's tail swatted me in the face and one foot punched Oma in the stomach as she tried to get up. Oma grunted. Nah'ee screeled in anger. Big red blotches almost blinded me and Bruyah covered her ears with her hands. The others jumped back, their eyes wide.

Kisin just lay there, stunned. "I touched a Great Dragon!" he said with a big grin on his face. Yochi hopped on Kisin's shoulder and chittered. Kisin stroked Yochi's neck and mind-talked. I couldn't hear what was said, but I knew he was telling Yochi that *he* was the most wonderful dragon, that Nah'ee was not as special. Dragons do need to be reassured sometimes.

Nah'ee stopped screeling and sat on her haunches. Her mouth kind of quivered and little squeaky cries came out. Her eyes were twirling red and purple. On Arald and Tahli, those colors mean anger or fear. I looked at Oma. She lifted one eyebrow and said something to Tahli.

"Nah'ee will sleep soon," Oma said. "We must make her calmer so she doesn't have bad dreams."

Kisin and I looked at each other. Our eyes got wide. Oh, yes. I sure hoped Nah'ee only had good dreams—always.

Ben and Arald and The Lost Baby Karel Henneberger

Tahli sat on a branch and talked to Nah'ee quietly in a humming sort of voice. Yochi stayed on Kisin's shoulder, humming softly.

I looked at the portal. Arald had been gone a long time. I thought about how the dragons had growled at us last year and almost threw flames at us. I swallowed, then remembered Arald was on Great Dragon business. The other dragons wouldn't hurt Arald. They wouldn't dare. Would they?

Just as I was getting really worried, Arald fell out of the portal *"Benmin-Arald go Dragon World! Eldest Great Dragon say!"* he shouted.

A lot of chittering came from all the dragons—too fast for me to follow. I got the gist, though. Yochi was mad that Arald was going to the Dragon World and he wasn't. Tahli wanted to know how and when. Arald tried to answer them both and began stuttering. I saw Polter come close enough to listen.

Oma patted Nah'ee, fed her more leaves, and called out to the dragons. They all turned and ducked their heads. Arald's nose was red. Tahli got a bit red, too. Yochi, however, just stood tall, his eyes glowing red.

Ben and Arald and The Lost Baby
Karel Henneberger

"Eldest Great Dragon say Benmin-Arald go Dragon World," Arald stated firmly, landing on my shoulder with a hard thump. He tucked his wings tight to his body. His eyes were swirling blue and green—colors that meant he was pleased and sure of himself—and surprised as well.

"How?" *"Can't get through." "Arald can. Not Ben."* Oma, Yochi, and Tahli said at the same time.

"Eldest Great Dragon say use dragon power. Go home," Arald said. He tipped his head up sharply. *"We go soon."*

"Dragon power?" Kisin asked. Yochi bent his neck and leaned forward. I don't think he was as pleased as Arald. His eyes swirled purple with some red.

Oma and Tahli had one of their silent conversations. I nudged Arald. He shrugged one shoulder. He couldn't hear them, either. "Why can Tahli always hear us?" I asked mentally.

Arald dipped his head. *"Tahli mother to Arald? Knows like Benmin mother?"*

I sighed and nodded. Then my brain caught up to what I'd heard. "What did you mean we go to the Dragon World by dragon power?" I asked him—not silently.

"Eldest Great Dragon say we go dragon power," he answered just as not silently. *"Not understand how,"* he added.

Oma and Tahli came over. Oma looked a bit worried. Tahli's eyes were first shuttered. The first eyelid on a dragon is almost transparent. It protects their eyes from dust and dirt while flying. It also hides emotions somewhat. Tahli was worried or knew something she didn't want to tell us.

Chapter Twelve—Orders

Oma stroked Arald's neck. "Arald, *exactly* what did the Eldest Great Dragon tell you?"

Arald calmed down a bit, then slipped off my shoulder and stood on a fallen tree trunk near the portal. *"Eldest Great Dragon say Benmin-Arald go Dragon World soon."* He was absolutely certain sure about *that*.

I sat down beside him. Oma knelt in front of us. Tahli stayed on her shoulder. "What *exact* words did the Eldest Great Dragon use?" Oma asked him again gently.

Arald dipped his head. His eyes swirled with reds, blues, and purple. He filled my head with big splobs of those colors, too.

Ben and Arald and The Lost Baby   Karel Henneberger

Red usually means danger or anger. Blue means something he knows well or is happy about. Those are pretty well set for meanings, though the shades of the colors can make a difference. But purple is generally something he's not sure of. A puzzle or something he's not confident he can do. Gradually, I saw more purple and blue than red.

"You're sure, but you're not sure?" I asked him.

Arald tipped his head up—yes. Then down—no. *"Can say words, but not meanings,"* He said.

"Too young. Not think enough," Polter said. He raised one foot and extended the claws.

Oma frowned at him, then back at Arald. "So just say the words as the Eldest Great Dragon said them to you," Oma said patiently.

Arald swallowed. So did I. Arald and I had pretty much perfected our communications. This confusion was new. Arald's head tipped down. *"Arald go alone to Dragon World. No Benmin. No Tahli. Words mean different."*

"So, when Tahli and I aren't with you, you don't understand what the Eldest Great Dragon says?" I asked him. "But you went there before without me."

"Not with no Tahli." Arald's nose was getting red.

"Don't be embarrassed, Arald. You're doing great," I told him, stroking his back.

He took a big breath, then said all at once, *"Little One go with Benmin to mountain place to find…"* Arald stopped and looked up at Oma. *"I don't know word,"* he said sadly. *"We go mountain place find something. Eldest Great Dragon say we will know. It has dragon power. It will let us go home. Then Benmin-Arald go Dragon World."*

"A mountain place," Oma said in a worried voice. "You will find someone…some*thing,*" she corrected herself. Arald nodded up. Yes. "Something that will get you home to Hidden Valley. Or take you?" she added uncertainly.

Arald nodded up several times. Yes. That is what he heard. *"Eldest Great Dragon say Benmin-Arald go mountain place, then home, then Dragon World,"* Arald rubbed his face against my cheek.

"But what is the mountain place we need to find?" I asked Oma.

Oma looked away, thinking. "Mountain place," she said slowly. Then, "Arald. Did she mean the place on the mountain where we spent the night?"

Arald's eyes opened wide. *"Mountain place. Mountain* food *place. Yes!"*

Oma grinned. "Of course. The Eldest Great Dragon would know Arald would remember food. You are to go to Myku's home."

I grinned, too. Well, that mystery was solved. Now we just had to find out what we were looking for.

Suddenly, Polter flew over to a tree branch near us. *"Polter go home with too young. Polter long away from Kembe. Polter not needed here more."*

I looked at Polter. He did seem a little…faded. Do dragons have to stay near their human partners or get sick? "Oma?"

"They *have* been apart much longer than is usual," Oma said with a frown. "Perhaps it is best that Polter go along with you and Arald after all."

Arald didn't look happy. *"Eldest Great Dragon not say Benmin-Arald, Polter go. Say Benmin-Arald go."*

"But he misses the Old Man…uh, Kembe," I said soothing down his crest. "Maybe Kembe needs him, too. I'd miss you if you were gone so long."

Arald dipped his head. He sighed. *"Arald miss Benmin, too. But Polter must tell Eldest Great Dragon is his idea,"* he added frowning at Polter.

Polter nodded. *"Eldest Great Dragon understand. Misses Baby."*

That made sense. "What dragons decree..." Oma said, raising one eyebrow at me.

I rolled my eyes. "...shall certainly be," I said, finishing the phrase.

While we had been involved with the Dragon World stuff, Yochi and Tahli were humming something that kept Nah'ee calm. Kisin was stroking her neck and grinning the biggest grin I've ever seen. The rest of the Koqui knelt with their hands over their eyes. Their fingers left only small spaces that let them see while still hiding behind their hands.

"Nah'ee sleeps soon," Tahli said quietly. *"We stay. We keep Terror away."*

Yochi snorted. *"I keep Quetzalcoatl's Child not afraid,"* He said, puffing out his chest and unfurling his wings.

I really didn't like him. He was probably jealous because Kisin was spending so much time with another dragon. A bigger dragon.

Oma eased over so she could talk to Kisin who was still feeding Baby Nah'ee. "Benjamin and Arald are commanded by the Eldest Great Dragon to go to the home of Myku. From there they will go to Hidden Valley, then through the portal there to the Dragon World."

"For what good?" Kisin asked, handing another armful of leaves to Nah'ee. "Nah'ee cannot go."

Oma shook her head. "I don't know yet. But Benjamin and Arald have gone to the Dragon World before and come back with advice and help for our world. They will need a guide to Myku's house."

Kisin beckoned Bruyah and said, "Go to the village. Bring back a guide." He waved her off. She glared at me, but set off back the way we'd come. Two of the guards went with her.

While Bruyah was gone, the rest of us split up to find more of the grey-green leaves Nah'ee seemed to like best. The dragons sat near her humming softly. Except for Polter, who apparently couldn't hum. He just rumbled. But Nah'ee seemed satisfied.

Finally, Nah'ee slid until her head was almost lying on Kisin's lap. Her eyes were only half open. Her feet stuck out awkwardly and her wings kind of splayed open. They weren't fully opened yet, but still each wing was as long as Arald's whole wingspan from tip to tip. Nah'ee was a BIG baby.

Yochi flew down to Kisin's shoulder and rubbed his neck against Kisin's cheek. Kisin smiled and eased back from Nah'ee. He stood, talking silently to Yochi. Polter, Arald, and Tahli continued to hum-rumble.

Bruyah and a short, broad man came along the path. He wasn't fat, just broad. Nah'ee could have sat on his shoulder easily. Arald stopped humming and flew to my shoulder. *"Man take us mountain food place?"* he asked.

"I guess so, Arald." We watched the pair come closer. Bruyah looked furious. Of course. Arald and I were going to the Dragon World and she wasn't.

The man wore a small pack. It was probably bigger than mine, but it looked small on him. "Young Manos-to-be said Kisin calls Ha-guy." His eyes darted about the clearing, going wide when he saw Nah'ee. He knelt down and bowed his head.

Chapter Thirteen—Down the Mountain

Kisin stepped forward. "We have found the source of the Terror—a child of the great Quetzalcoatl. She cannot find her way to the world where her mother lives. It is for you to guide this one," he said, pointing to me, "and these Quetzal Children," he added waving a hand toward Polter and Arald, "to the house of Myku. There you guide them, then here return."

The man bowed his head twice, then looked at me and Arald with eyes almost as wide as when he had seen Nah'ee.

He stood. "We now go?" he asked, though I'm not sure if he was asking me or Kisin or Oma.

Oma nodded. "I think it would be best to do the Eldest Great Dragon's bidding quickly." She put her arms around both me and Arald. "You will do well. Both of you," she said quietly. She stroked Arald's back and smoothed my hair, then stood back. She nodded sharply.

I don't remember much about the next few minutes. I know Oma fetched my pack. I know Yochi stood proudly on Kisin's shoulder. And I remember Bruyah watched Nah'ee and turned to me and sneered. Then Arald and I were following Ha-guy and one of the armed men was behind us. I looked around for Polter, but didn't see him.

"Polter near," Arald said. *"He follows."*

"Why do we need the guard?" I asked out loud.

The guide stopped, turned, and bowed to me—or maybe to Arald. Or both of us, I guess. "Jungle has dangers," he said, not *quite* looking at me or Arald.

"I thought the animals are afraid of us," I asked Arald silently, remembering Oma's advice about listening ears.

"Animals afraid. Men not know. They guard."

"Oh. Well, it's only until we get to Myku's house," I thought to him.

Ben and Arald and The Lost Baby

Karel Henneberger

"Then we find thing take us home?" Arald asked, twisting his head to look at my face.

I sighed. "I certainly hope so. Any idea what 'it' is?"

Arald tilted his head. He was asking Tahli. He shrugged. *"Not know. Tahli not know. Not ask Yochi. Not ask Polter."*

"Maybe Polter would know. He's much older and has been to the Dragon World recently," I muttered to Arald, thinking as I went.

Arald went quiet for a minute. Then, Polter flew down beside us. The men both jumped and spun about. The guard drew his sword-thing and started to swing it at Polter. "WAIT!" I yelled. "It's just Polter—another dragon—a Quetzal Child," I added quickly.

The guard threw down his weapon and cowered on the ground. Afraid, I guess that Polter or Arald would attack him. Even Ha-guy was kneeling with his face in his hands, just as scared.

"Said not old enough. Won't do. Not think enough." Polter said.

"Grouchy old one," Arald whispered to me, then stood as tall as he could.

I almost smiled. But we did need whatever Polter could tell us. "So, Polter, dragon-bound to the Old Man, do you know what we are to look for?" I asked as politely as I could.

"Hmmph. Polter partner to Kembe. We know much. Find Big Empty. Great Dragons trust Kembe. Trust Polter." Polter puffed out his chest proudly.

"You found the Big Empty? What is it?" I asked excitedly. After all, last year Arald and I had stopped the Big Empty when it invaded our world. We deserved to know what it was.

"Not tell now. Too young. Ask question needed," Polter said, glaring at me.

"Yeah." I drew in a big breath. "Okay. Do you know what the thing is that Arald and I need to find at Myku's house? The thing that will take us home?"

Polter was quiet for a long minute. He looked at the jungle around us. He frowned down at the two men shaking at our feet. He seemed to shrink down to about half size. He sighed. *"Polter cannot know what. Only know Hard. Carved."* He stopped. He looked at me. He looked at Arald. Then he flew off into the trees without another word.

"Well. A hard, carved something," I said out loud. "Not sure that helps a lot."

Arald nodded, then grinned. *"Polter knows not much."*

I nodded, but thought of what Polter had said. And what he hadn't said. "He does know a lot. He knows about the Big Empty. Just not this. How did he know *anything* about this, though?" I thought to Arald.

Arald flicked his tail. *"What dragons decree…?"*

I nodded. "…shall certainly be. Well, the Eldest Great Dragon wants her Baby home. I think she'll make sure we can do what we have to."

The men stood and bowed to me and Arald and we started back down the trail. The guard—I never did hear his name—bowed, picked up his weapon and followed us. Neither man would look directly at us. It was a silent trip down the mountain—well, half way down the mountain. We came to the two stone pillars just as it was getting dark. A light was coming toward us. Myku.

Ha-guy held out his hand. Myku did the same. They exchanged small bags of something. I remembered Myku and Kisin had done the same. Myku saw me watching and smiled. "We are both Kocqui. When Kocqui meet, we exchange packets of coffee beans. It is our way of showing respect. I married outside the Kocqui, but I am still Kocqui."

The men bowed to Arald and me, turned and headed back up the mountain.

"Myku," I said, starting to ask if he knew what we were looking for.

"Myku only on other side of Black Line by pillars. Not Myku here. Myku means 'in between' in Kocqui. Bogado, Little Brother name for same. I work between Kocqui and Little Brothers in the valleys."

He stopped just before we reached his house. "My wife knows not of the Quetzal Children. I know. My grandfather is Manos and joined with a Quetzal Child, Yochi." He paused, glancing quickly at Arald. "Perhaps this Quetzal Child will hide as before?" he asked hesitantly.

"Of course," I said. "Arald? Please?"

Bogado's eyes grew wide and I could see his knees bend a little when the dragon on my shoulder suddenly wasn't there. He drew a shaky breath, swallowed, and walked toward the house.

Once there, Señora Maria smiled and offered me a large bowl of stew and some of the pastries Arald liked so much. "Do like we did at home," I told him silently.

I felt him slip under the table and curl his tail around my foot. That way I knew where he was and his tail couldn't get stepped on. I slipped him part of a pastry. "Not so loud, Arald. Chew quietly, please."

"Hungry. More?"

I ate the stew, while Arald gulped down all of the pastries. Señor Bogado showed me the bed where Oma and I had slept. "In morning, wife, I go market. You be here. Stay, follow, as needed. We return before dark."

"Gracias, Señor Bogado," I said. I had been wondering how we'd be able to search for the hard, carved thing we needed without them seeing us. He bowed, glancing at my shoulder. Arald blinked into view for a second, then blinked back neutral. Señor Bogado grinned and bowed again.

"Where's Polter?" I asked Arald.

In my head, I heard Polter say, *"Polter stay in trees. Too many humans."*

"Okay, Polter. See you in the morning," I told him silently.

"Polter sad," Arald said softly.

Ben and Arald and The Lost Baby Karel Henneberger

"Yes. He misses the Old Man...Kembe. And I guess he's not used to being around so many people anymore."

"If Benmin long away, Arald miss, too," Arald said silently to me so Polter couldn't hear.

I nodded. "Me, too."

The Black
Line

Chapter Fourteen—The Search

Morning came. Señora Maria served us meat wrapped in some kind of flat dough. Not tortillas, but not bread either. They were good, spicy but good. I ate three and Arald had four. Señora Maria seemed happy I had such a good appetite.

I helped Señor Bogado pack both mules. I don't know what he told his wife about me staying, but they headed down the mountain, leaving Arald and me—and Polter—behind.

"Okay. Where do we start looking?" I asked Arald. "Not inside the house, I hope."

Arald shrugged. *"Maybe trail?"*

"Well, it's worth a try. Let's start at those pillars," I suggested. "The weird stuff didn't show up until we were past them, so…"

Arald flew off and Polter swooped after him. I went slower, looking around for anything hard and carved. *"Here!"* Arald called excitedly.

I hurried ahead. The stone pillar on the right had something carved on it. Moss almost covered it, but there was something there. I opened the screwdriver part of my knife and began scraping at the moss. Arald pulled the pieces free. One whole side was covered with lines chiseled into the stone. It might once have been a picture, but time had worn away most of it.

"I can't make out what it is," I said, sitting back on my heels. I tried tracing one line with my finger. It seemed to want to join with another line, but that part was pretty much gone. "I hope this isn't what we're looking for because I'm just not getting anything," I said to Arald.

"Other pillar maybe," Polter said from where he sat on a fallen log.

"Yeah. Good idea," I told him. I started to walk across the path to the other pillar when I noticed the black line connecting them. Had that been there before? Maybe the light was just right now that the sun was high.

"Short man said Black Line border," Arald said, twisting his head this way and that. The Black Line was a handspan wide and seemed to start under the pillar I'd been working on, continued across the pathway and dipped under the other pillar.

I walked around to the other side and saw that the Black Line went on into the jungle. "The Black Line. A divider between the Little Brothers' world and the Kocqui, maybe. But what makes it?" I dug my toe across the line. Not dirt. Kneeling, I touched it with my fingers. Warm. I moved my hand to the dirt right beside the Line. That felt like dirt. But the Black Line was different. It was smooth, not hard, not soft, but warm.

"Dragon power?" Arald asked.

"I don't know. Something different, anyway." My hand wanted to follow the line into the jungle. "I'm going to follow it for a bit. See what happens. Don't let me get lost," I said to Arald and Polter.

"Not get lost," Arald said. *"Follow line only."*

I crouched down and let my right hand glide over the Black Line. I had to start crawling to keep in touch with it and my knees were soon wet with jungle damp. The Black Line wasn't going in a straight line, I noticed. It went down when the ground went up and up when the ground went down. "It's following the altitude line, I think."

"Line marks above big water," Polter said, nodding. *"Too young. Think only some. Maybe do."*

"A compliment from Polter?" I asked Arald silently. He just grinned.

"Hmmph. Boy follow line," Polter said.

I followed the Line for what seemed like a mile. I looked back and could just see the second pillar, so I really hadn't gone far. I looked ahead and sighed. The Line seemed warmer as if it wanted me to keep going.

Just when I was getting hungry and my knees were starting to complain, the Line went under a rock. I moved around to the other side of the rock, and the Line continued. The rock was about the size of my head. Maybe it had fallen on the Line. When I laid my hand back on the Line, it wasn't as warm as before. I sat back. Warmer meant on the right track? Cooler meant I missed something?

"Maybe under rock?" Arald suggested.

Ben and Arald and The Lost Baby

Karel Henneberger

I shrugged. As good an idea as any. I picked up the rock. Or tried to. It was heavy! Much heavier than a rock that size should be. I tried rolling it off the Line. No luck. It moved, so it wasn't dug into the ground. It just didn't want to move away from the Line.

Polter flew down to stand beside the rock. He cocked his head and said, *"Move on Line?"*

I tried pushing it over. "Nope." I stood and looked down at it. There was something different about this rock. "Maybe if we all try pushing it."

Polter and Arald pushed with their heads while I shoved with my arms, bracing myself with my legs. No good.

"Other way?" Arald said with a bit of a huff.

We all got on the other side of the rock and tried again. It moved. "Push against the top," I said. We tried once more.

"It moves!" *"Works!"* Arald and Polter both said together. We grinned at each other, then looked down at the rock.

It now lay on its side, along the Black Line. The exposed side was hard to see, but there was something carved on it. I had to almost lie down to see what it was. "Some kind of picture, I think," I said finally, brushing my hand across the engraving. A tingle went up my arm and somehow I knew what was carved there. "It's a shell and a spider."

I put my whole hand on the carving and closed my eyes. "It's the First Mother." How did I know that? The carved shell glowed a bright blue-green. The spider's legs moved to curl around the edges of the carving.

The tingle turned into a jolt that ran up my arm and into my head. Not like the jackhammer of the Terror. More like when I touched both poles of a battery. I jerked my hand away and rocked backwards, landing on my backside.

"Benmin okay?" Arald said, coming to my side.

"Boy hurt?" Polter added, coming to my other side.

"Not hurt. I don't think so, anyway," I assured them. "But I think we've found what will take us home."

"How." That was Polter.

"When?" That was Arald.

"Oma said sooner would be better. I guess now?" I said, not really sure.

"How?" Polter said again.

Ben and Arald and The Lost Baby

We stood there looking down at the rock. "Well, we're supposed to go together, so maybe we need to touch the carving on the rock at the same time?" I said almost as a question.

Arald and Polter looked at each other. They looked at me. They both nodded. So did I. I knelt down again and drew in a big breath. "Okay. We touch the rock at the same time. Arald, you get on my shoulder. That way you'll be touching it when I do. Polter, you lean against me so we're touching, too. Then I'll put both hands on the rock and think 'home.' I hope that works."

I felt like clicking my heels, but I didn't have red shoes and we didn't want to go to Kansas, anyway. I shook my head. Stop thinking about the *Wizard of Oz*, I told myself, and start thinking of Hidden Valley.

We got into position and I moved my hands until they were just an inch above the rock. "Ready?" I asked the dragons. Two nods. One more deep breath and I lowered my hands until they were flat on the rock, covering the shell with the moving spider carving. "Home," I said silently, then out loud, "Hidden Valley." I closed my eyes.

Chapter Fifteen—To the Dragon World

I expected another electrical zap and maybe spinning around like a tornado or something. Instead, I suddenly felt grass under my knees. No spinning, not even like the time Oma had moved across Hidden Valley in her rocking chair when we discovered the Big Empty invading our world. Dragon Power, she'd said. There was need. Then, leaves had swirled around her and the chair and she had to pat her hair back into place.

Polter moved away and Arald flipped his wings open. I opened my eyes. We were home. No zing. No spin. Just home.

Ben and Arald and The Lost Baby   Karel Henneberger

Polter immediately moved forward and took off. West. We were right beside Qua-nya-tse-né, the big green-gray rock in the middle of Hidden Valley. Oma said the Great Dragons must have moved it here from the only other place it's found on earth—in Northwestern Canada—to guard the Valley from intruders. It's really a kind of Gneiss, a volcanic rock over four billion years old. The original peoples called it The Great Green Rock of God and it is impressive. Big. Very big. And hard. Last year we'd needed a piece to help make the paste that kept the Big Empty from destroying our world. It was all Dad could do to chip off a hand-sized chunk.

Right now, the important thing was that Qua-nya-tse-né was right in the middle of the Valley. We had a long walk ahead of us to get to the portal on the western side of the Valley. Well, I had a long walk. Arald could have flown it in minutes, but he stayed nearby as I plodded along.

We were both hungry. Arald found lots of bugs and things to eat, but there wasn't much ripe fruit yet for me. We'd spent all morning finding the hard, carved thing Polter had told us about, so it was past noon. An hour to the western cliff, then into the Dragon World and who knew how long we'd be staying there. I sighed, looking back at Oma's house on the top of the Eastern edge of the Valley. There was food there, but it would take several hours to get there, eat, then hike all the way across the Valley to the portal.

"Dragon beans taste good," Arald said.

"I'm sure, but you think bugs are tasty," I told him. I sighed and kept on walking, hoping that the dragons would decree that I get something to eat.

Finally, we got to the slope leading to the cliff where the portal was. Looking back, I could see Smudge, the Valley's resident bear, working his way back home. His cave is really just some flat rocks tilted to make a teepee-shaped cave. I remembered Dad had said there was a surprise just outside it. So, as long as Smudge wasn't there to be bothered, I looked around for something I hadn't noticed last year.

We climbed—well, I climbed and Arald flew—to just above Smudge's cave and started moving along the narrow path toward the portal. And there, just about my eye height, was a heart chipped into the rock. There was a J.D. then a plus sign, then A.A. inside the heart. James Drake + Anna Andrews. Mom and Dad. I traced the letters with one finger, scraping off some lichen that had grown there. Maybe last year Dad had been going to tell me that Mom knew about dragons. Instead, we'd gotten caught up with the Big Empty.

Arald chittered and I came back to today. *"Portal near,"* Arald chittered again. I sighed, wiped my hand on my pants and set off again.

"I'm coming, Arald. How long have you known that Mom knew about you?" I asked him as I eased my way around a particularly tight corner.

"Dragons say time right," he said.

"What dragons? Tahli? The Great Dragons?"

Arald shrugged. *"Tahli say dragons say yes. Great Dragons, maybe? Others?"*

"Well, they could have told me, too," I mumbled

And we were there. I looked at the faint zig-zag mark on the cliff. I drew in a big breath. Arald and I had gone to the Dragon World more than once, but I wasn't really looking forward to another visit. Arald landed on my shoulder and put his check against mine. *"Dragons nice last time."*

"Yeah, but you were alone. They don't like humans." I puffed out a big breath. "Here we go," I said silently. I leaned into the cliff.

I felt like we were standing still, but the light from the other side—the Dragon World side—grew brighter. Then we were on the ledge above a crowd of dragons and wyverns. Always before, Arose had been there to take us to the Great Dragons' counsel place. This time there were only all those dragons below us with their long dragon teeth.

"Welcome. You must be Arald."

I turned and saw a very old man leaning on a long staff. Polter sat on his shoulder, looking as sour as ever. Arald chirped a 'hello.' *"Oma's Old Man and Polter,"* he said silently.

"Kembe," I corrected him.

"It matters not," the old man—Kembe—said. "Azzie knew me as the Old Man. I'd almost forgotten what my call name had been. Polter remembered. I was Old Man then and even Older Man now." He gave a half-bow. "And you are…" he asked me.

"I am Benjamin Thomas Drake, dragon-bound to Arald since last year." I bowed back.

"Ah, yes. Polter neglected to say your name." He tilted his head to look at Polter.

"Too young. Maybe think," Polter said, glaring at us.

I smiled. 'Maybe think' was a real compliment coming from him. But he still said we were too young. "What are we too young for?" I asked.

Just then, Arose and another dragon hovered beside the ledge. *"Young Hoomun, Arald come,"* Arose said, dropping his neck so we could climb on. *"Chobah take Old Man Hoomun, Polter."*

It didn't seem as though the dragons below us were quite as ferocious looking this time. Polter had said that they trusted the Old Man—uh, Kembe. I guess I got lumped in with some of that trust. While he was with me, anyway.

We landed on a wide flat spot on a high ledge. Eldest Great Dragon was there. So was Taranoka, the one dragon who was willing to say he was a friend to hoomuns. I bowed to the Eldest Great Dragon first, then to Taranoka, then to the third Great Dragon who had never talked when we were there before.

"Kembe. Polter. And well come to Young Arald and Pennamin," the Eldest Great Dragon said.

Apparently, Great Dragons can't say the B or J sound. I almost grinned, but then thought how hard it was for me to pronounce the Spanish dar prisa correctly. And I didn't have a mouthful of humungous teeth to speak through.

"You come with news of my child?"

"Yes, Eldest Great Dragon," I said bowing again. "Nah'ee is eating well. She is afraid. I think she's confused that she can hear you, but not see you."

"Yes." The Eldest Great Dragon tipped her head up. *"The portal is too small there. Nah'ee must come through the portal in Hidden Valley."*

"How will we get her there? I know she won't leave the portal in Colombia." I said, thinking of how Nah'ee had gotten stuck in that portal. It took three of us to pull her out. She didn't want to leave there. It was the closest she could come to her mother. I wouldn't want to have to try to get her to go with us to the Black Line Rock.

"Yes. Nah'ee hatchling. Nah'ee not understand. You take what is needed. Bring Nah'ee here." She flicked a claw towards the third Great Dragon.

He flew off with a wild flap of his wings. The disturbed air made me rock back on my heels. Arald lifted a bit until I was steady again, then he sat back on my shoulder.

The Eldest Great Dragon leaned back, curled her tail around her legs and closed her eyes. We waited.

Chapter Sixteen—Three Threes

"Hungry." Arald said silently.

"Yeah. Me, too. We'll just have to wait." I stroked Arald's back to keep him calm. Waiting isn't his best quality. It's not mine, either.

Kembe drew out a small pouch. "Dragon beans. Good to eat," he said, taking one out and biting a piece. He held the pouch out to me, jiggling it to show there were more beans inside.

I opened the pouch and pulled out two strange-looking beans. Each was as long as my little finger and as wide as my thumb. They were thicker than potato chips, but not quite cracker thick. I couldn't quite decide what color they were. Colors in the

Dragon World are weird. Not just being dragon-bound weird, but more 'touching a rock in Colombia and appearing in Hidden Valley' weird. I could taste some colors and almost hear others.

Arald dipped his head and grabbed one from my hand, chewing loudly. "Arald!"

"Hungry," he said silently since his mouth was full of bean. I took a small bite of the bean left in my hand. Not bad. Didn't taste like beans at all. More like…chocolate marshmallow? I took a bigger bite. Yeah. Chocolate marshmallow.

"Thanks, Kembe," I said, as soon as I swallowed.

Polter sat on his shoulder and frowned. *"Too young. Eat too much. Not ready."*

I sighed and took another bite of the Dragon bean so I wouldn't say something I shouldn't.

"Dragons forget humans have to eat more often than they do." Kembe said, grinning.

Flapping wings—big wings—told us that the third Great Dragon was back. He held a piece of log in his front claws. I braced myself. Once his back feet were on the ground, he settled his wings. He leaned forward and plopped the log piece in front of me, then moved to stand behind the Eldest Great Dragon.

Ben and Arald and The Lost Baby Karel Henneberger

I looked at the log. It wasn't just a log. It had a piece of bark on top and a kind of handle attached. "A bucket?" I thought to Arald.

"Log bucket?" he answered silently.

"It is a kind of bucket," Kembe said with a smile. Polter just grunted. Probably thinking we weren't old enough to know what a bucket is. "Dragons have no need for buckets, but I have. I've taught them how to make quite a few things since I must live here. They treat them like toys." He grinned.

The Eldest Great Dragon smiled—I think. That was kind of scary. She has a lot of teeth, though she wasn't showing them much, so I guessed it was a smile. *"Take where Nah'ee is. Use water to make drink for her."* She flicked a claw at Taranoka.

"Nah'ee heir of the Eldest Great Dragon. To bring her here, three threes must you have," he said in his low, growly voice. *"First three: Three dragons. Second three: Three hoomuns dragon-bound. Last Three: Part of Nah'ee future, part of Nah'ee present, and part of Nah'ee past."* Taranoka bowed to the Eldest Great Dragon, then to Arald and me.

"The Dragon World water is Nah'ee future?" I asked. The Eldest Great Dragon tilted her head up and back. Dragon for 'yes.'

"But what is part of her present and past?" I wondered out loud.

"Nah'ee past is shell of Nah'ee egg. Must grind, add to water," Taranoka explained.

"Nah'ee present be Nah'ee place now." The Eldest Great Dragon, clicked two claws together.

Taranoka continued, *"Power part of three dragons, three dragon-bound hoomuns in Nah'ee place now. With Nah'ee shell, make drink for Nah'ee."*

"I think the Power part means feathers and hair," Kembe said, hesitantly. "Hair or scales and claws are used in many of the dragon's potions. They give…" he hesitated, "they give personality and power to the potion."

The Eldest Great Dragon tipped her head up. Yes.

I looked at Eldest Great Dragon and bowed again. I wanted to make sure I had the recipe right. "We need to take this bucket of Dragon World water, grind the egg shell, take feathers and fur or hair from each dragon and dragon-bound human, and mix them all together. Yes?"

"Pennamin say true. Must all Power pieces mix same time, but separate. Make warm. Not hot," she added quickly. *"Warm. Nah'ee drink."* She flicked her claw at Taranoka again.

"Then Arald, Penniman bring Nah'ee home same way as now," he told us.

I nodded. Arald chirped. Arose arrived. Chobah didn't. I looked at Kembe.

"I must stay here," Kembe said a bit sadly. "I can no longer go through the portal. Polter and I remain in this world."

I bowed to the three Great Dragons with an extra low bow to Eldest Great Dragon, then a nod to Kembe and Polter. I picked up the log bucket—the heavy log bucket—and...had a thought. "Uh. Eldest Great Dragon?"

She had been turning away, but twisted her head back to say, *"Yes. Young Pennamin has need?"*

"Uh. How are we supposed to get back to Colombia—to where Nah'ee is?"

Eldest Great Dragon's nose changed color. If it had been Arald, I'd have thought she was embarrassed. *"An important need, certainly,"* she said with a kind of chuckle. *"Return to the Great*

Green Rock that guards your valley. Together do as you did at the Black Line Rock. You will be there. Return with Nah'ee same way."

"Thank you," I said with another low bow. Then, I somehow managed to climb onto Arose without spilling any water from the log bucket. We flew quickly to the ledge in the cliff where the portal was. There were quite a few dragons there, but none were rumbling or flashing teeth. They weren't smiling, either, but they weren't threatening to breathe fire, so…

Carefully, I slid down the Arose's neck to the ledge. Arald chirped. I bowed. Arose nodded and with one flap of his wings, headed back the way we'd come.

"Well, Arald," I said, setting the bucket down for a minute. "We have the recipe. Now all we have to do is go back to Colombia, find what's left of the egg shell after Nah'ee hatched, pull out some feathers from Yochi and some hairs from Kisin, Oma, me, you and Tahli, and mix them up with this water."

"She must drink," Arald added.

"Oh, yes. I hope she likes the taste." I picked the bucket up again. It was still heavy.

Just as we reached the dark zigzag scar on the cliff wall, I remembered I'd forgotten to ask Kembe about the Big Empty. *"Next time,"* Arald said.

I was hoping there wouldn't be a next time. But now we had to get back to our world. I had learned not to lean too hard going into the portal. You tend to come out just as hard. So I just eased in slowly and managed to keep my footing when we came out into Hidden Valley.

The Black Line Rock

Chapter Seventeen—Back to Colombia

Most of the Valley was in shadow. Only the eastern cliff was still sunlit. I sighed. Almost an hour's walk back to Qua-nya-tse-né. Probably more with the log bucket to carry. Arald flitted ahead to drink from Long Creek that ran through the middle of the Valley from north to south.

"Too bad Bracken isn't here," I said, looking down at the rocky pathway. Bracken is a mule who comes when needed. Apparently, the dragons didn't think he was needed right now.

Hiking down the steep path to Hidden Valley itself isn't bad. Unless you're carrying a heavy log bucket filled with unreplaceable water from the Dragon World. Even with the switchbacks that made the path less steep, I had a tough time.

Ben and Arald and The Lost Baby

Karel Henneberger

"Sure glad I joined the strength training club last winter," I muttered. With Arald growing and me getting taller, Dad had said I needed to get my muscles and joints in shape. I kind of liked doing the exercises, but this was definitely not as enjoyable.

Arald flew back and sat on a rock. *"Benmin strong now. Arald strong too."*

I set the bucket down and stretched. "Yeah, we're both a lot stronger than we were last year. You were just a hatchling like Nah'ee and I was barely in middle school yet."

"Arald not like Nah'ee. Nah'ee never sit on shoulder," Arald said proudly.

"Arald ate like Nah'ee, though," I told him, holding out the bag of Dragon beans.

"Hmph," He said, snatching a bean with one claw.

I pulled out a bean, too, and licked. Not chocolate marshmallow. More like banana cream pie. "We'll have to get some of these for Mom and Dad," I said, nibbling around the edges of the bean before chomping off a big piece.

"Said Dragon beans taste good," Arald said silently. Being able to talk without speaking is great when your mouth is full.

I stuffed the rest of the Dragon bean in my mouth, picked up the bucket, and started on down into the Valley. "You did say they taste good, but our tastes aren't always the same," I reminded him.

"Benmin like fuzzy juice," he said, wrinkling his forehead. He didn't like sodas.

"Arald likes bugs," I said back, wrinkling my nose.

Finally, I was on the Valley floor and I hadn't spilled any Dragon water. The trip down from the cliffside had taken twice as long as usual. "Now an easy hike to Qua-nya-tse-né," I said. I stood as straight as I could while lifting the log bucket. The shadow was almost halfway up the eastern cliffside. "We should make it before dark," I told Arald.

"Then quick to Black Line Rock," he answered. *"How to find path?"* he added.

I thought a bit. It was more awkward walking with the log bucket on level ground. "Maybe Myku can take us." It was slow going, but Arald kept me occupied with his chatter.

"We sleep at mountain food place?" Arald asked, his tongue slipping across his lips.

Ben and Arald and The Lost Baby Karel Henneberger

"We'll see," I panted. Not much farther. But how to cross the stream. It wasn't deep where it went around Qua-nya-tse-né, but the stepping stones could be slippery. "Too bad the dragons didn't decree an easier way to get back," I said with a sigh.

Arald flew ahead, then across Long Creek and back to where I was slogging along the trail. *"Stones dry. Can cross with bucket."*

I stopped and hefted the log bucket up with my other hand. "Okay," I told him. "Not far now. We'll make it before dark. I hope."

"Arald could help. Carry Dragon beans," he said slyly.

I grinned. "Oh no. There wouldn't be any left by the time I got over Long Creek."

Arald dipped his head. His nose was a bit pink. *"Arald only eat some,"* he assured me.

"We can each have one when we get to Black Line Rock," I told him. That gave us both something to look forward to.

After a few years or minutes, I stepped from the last stone to solid ground. I bent over, prying the bucket handle from my fingers, and flopped back.

"Need to touch Dragon Rock," Arald reminded me as he landed beside the bucket.

"Dragon Rock. Is that what you call Qua-nya-tse-né?" I asked him.

"Long name. Rock brought by dragons." He shrugged. *"Dragon Rock."*

"Makes sense to me," I said, sitting up. I struggled to my feet and lifted the log bucket again. "Let's do it."

I stood in front of Qua-nya-tse-né—Dragon Rock. How to hold the bucket and put both hands on the rock? *"Maybe not hold bucket?"* Arald suggested.

"Was the ground even at Black Line Rock?" I asked him.

Arald tilted his head up, then down. *"Maybe?"* he answered. I saw purple blotches. He wasn't sure.

"Me, either. Well, I can't put both hands on the rock *and* hold the bucket," I decided.

"Both hands must be on rock?" Arald asked, cocking his head to one side.

I tilted my head, too. "Not sure," I said after thinking a bit. "I don't know why, but it feels right to use both hands."

Ben and Arald and The Lost Baby

Karel Henneberger

"Two hands right, then," Arald said. *"Maybe Great Dragons say?"* he added with purple overtones.

"Well, just to be sure…" I stood with my feet far enough apart so the bucket was between them and squeezed with my legs in case the ground wasn't level when we landed in Colombia. Arald sat on my shoulder. I placed both hands flat on the rock. "Colombia," I thought, then "Black Line Rock," I said out loud.

This time there was a kind of electric zing. "Different kinds of rock, maybe?" I thought to Arald. He shrugged. I looked around. Dark had already come to the dense jungle. I couldn't see the Black Line Rock, let alone try to follow the Line back to the pillars and down to Myku's place.

Just then we saw a light bobbing up the pathway. "Myku?" I called.

"Bogado here. Follow light. You stay our house tonight." He waved the lamp, which seemed brighter than it had. I could see the ground in front of me now.

Carefully, I lifted the log bucket and stepped forward. We weren't far from the pillars really, so it didn't take long to get to Señor Bogado.

"What you bring, leave here," he said.

I set the bucket beside the pillar with the carving. "Will it be safe here?" I asked, worried that some animal would decide to drink the Dragon water.

"All safe between pillars," he said, nodding. Then he turned and headed back down the path to his house. I hurried to follow him. Near the house, Señor Bogado looked at Arald, then at me.

"Arald?" I said. Señor Bogado grinned as Arald went neutral, then peeped one winking eye out and disappeared again. "Show off," I said. Arald was really getting the hang of that skill.

Inside, Señora Maria smiled and waved me to the table where a pile of her crusty pastries lay inviting us to eat.

With Arald at my feet, we finished every one. Dragon beans taste good, but they aren't very filling.

Chapter Eighteen—The Third Three

Early the next morning—after one of Señora Maria's breakfasts—we headed to the pillars with the larger mule. I picked up the log bucket and managed to hold it in place while Señor Bogado put a counterbalance on the other side of the mule. After some experimenting, we found that I had to keep a hand on the bucket or the mule stopped. Arald tried sitting on it, but that wasn't what the bucket wanted. "Dragons!" I thought. "They could make things easier."

"Now I be Myku," Señor Bogado told me as he passed between the pillars. "We meet guide. You follow guide to Mamos."

I nodded. Okay. I felt that tingle that meant Nah'ee was awake and not too far away. I wanted to get the Dragon World water there as soon as possible. "We still have to find the egg shell," I thought to Arald.

"Girl, Kisin know where?" he thought back.

"Maybe. They did say it was a sacred stone to them. Maybe they kept the pieces," I said. The trail was narrow and I had to walk beside the mule to keep my hand on the bucket. That meant lots of brush and spots with mud or rocks. The mule walked at his own pace. Steeper places didn't seem to make him slow down, but he didn't speed up on the even parts, either. It was slow going, but lots easier than carrying the bucket uphill.

Just as I was thinking we'd lost the way, Ha-guy and a guard appeared in front of us. They and Myku exchanged small bags of coffee beans as usual. Together we managed to untie the log bucket and lower it to the ground. I sat down on a convenient rock. Walking beside a mule on a narrow trail and holding onto a bucket is tiring.

Ben and Arald and The Lost Baby   Karel Henneberger

Myku turned and led the mule back down the mountain. No goodbye or see you later. Just turn and go. Very dragony of him. I sighed and heaved the bucket up again. Ha-guy led the way. Arald swooped through the trees. He was soon joined by Tahli. They played 'who can come closest to a tree and not hit it' for a while. I think Tahli won. *"Arald wings not work right,"* he said sadly.

I looked at him as he sat on a log in front of me. He had grown in the last few months. Bigger wings, bigger body. "You need to learn how to use your bigger body now," I told him.

Tahli nodded. *"Growing changes how to fly,"* she told him silently. *"Soon learn."*

By the time I'd worn out both arms a couple of times, we could hear Kisin directing his people. Nah'ee was hungry. So was I and it wasn't all just *her* hunger I felt. It had been a long time since breakfast.

"Hungry?" Arald said silently, remembering we were not supposed to speak out loud where Kisin or Bruyah or others could hear us. Something was not right about Bruyah. Better to talk silently.

"Yeah. Nah'ee is hungry, but so are we." I set the bucket down and pulled out the bag of Dragon beans. "Here, have one of these," I told him. "They should help our stomachs. We can only hope Nah'ee is well fed, too."

Just then, Oma came striding towards us. "Benjamin! Arald! You made good time," she said to us aloud. Silently, she added, "We're running out of the grey-green leaves Nah'ee wants."

She tried to take the bucket, but it wouldn't go. "It seems to want me to touch it," I explained.

"Well then, come and tell us what the Great Dragons decided." Oma walked beside me, leaning a bit so she could help hold the bucket's handle. I noticed that she didn't have to stoop much. I had grown bigger, too.

A few minutes later, Arald and I were standing in the open place near the portal. Kisin and Bruyah were feeding Nah'ee. Yochi was sitting on a branch humming to keep her calm. Tahli joined him. Soon the double humming did its job. Nah'ee slumped

Kisin rose and gestured with his staff for his people to sit in a C-shaped almost-circle with Nah'ee at the open end. Gently, he tapped his staff on the ground twice. Bruyah stood by his side. Oma was behind me.

"Speak, Young Dragon-bound to young Quetzal Child. What say the Great Dragons?" Kisin said in a quiet voice. Afraid to wake up Nah'ee, I guess.

"I bring water from the Dragon World, Kisin, dragon-bound to Yochi," I said in a voice a bit louder than Kisin's. We'd need help and the only ones who could help were in this circle, so they needed to hear, too.

I heard gasps and some whispers from the men in the circle. "Dragon World."

"The Eldest Great Dragon, mother of Nah'ee, told me what is needed to have her join her mother in the Dragon World." More gasps and whispers. Bruyah glared at me.

"Girl smell angry," Arald thought to me. *"Not want Nah'ee go."*

"Tough," I thought back. "What dragons decree…" I looked back at Oma. She nodded for me to go on.

"There are three threes we must have to make a potion that will allow us to take her to the Dragon World." I drew in a big breath. "The first three needed is three dragons. The second three is three dragon-bound humans. The third three has three parts." I paused. "Great Dragons like the number three," I explained.

I swallowed a couple of times. This part I had to get right. "We need part of Nah'ee past, part of Nah'ee present, and part of Nah'ee future." I stopped.

Kisin looked puzzled. Bruyah looked even angrier than before. Yochi flew to Kisin's shoulder. *"Young dragon-bound speaks not clearly,"* he said with a bit of a sneer.

"That is how it was said to us," I told them all. "It was also explained. "Nah'ee past is her shell. Nah'ee present is those where she is now. Three dragons—Yochi, Tahli, and Arald—and three dragon-bound humans—Oma, Kisin, and me. Nah'ee future is Dragon World water."

Oma nodded. "So, we have to find her shell and mix it with the other two parts?" she asked me. I nodded.

"We know where shell is," Kisin said, his face looking less worried. He waved to one of the guards. "Go with Bruyah. Bring back the pieces of the Sacred Stone."

Bruyah obviously didn't want to leave. I sighed. As much as I would enjoy her being banished, she really did need to know the whole thing.

"Bruyah should hear the rest of the orders," I told Kisin. He nodded and Bruyah and the guard sat back down. "The part of the dragons and dragon-bound is hair or feathers. They add Power and must be put into the potion at the same time, but separate.

Eldest Great Dragon said MUST. So we have to make sure those are put in at the same time."

"So feathers from Yochi, hair from Tahli and Arald," Oma said. "That's the parts of the dragons?" Arald and I nodded. "Then hair from Kisin, me, and Benjamin?" she continued. We nodded again. "All at the same time, but separate." She touched her hair, then nodded and stood even straighter. "We put these in at the same time, but each of us must drop our own part," she said, but not as a question.

Arald and I probably looked like bobble-heads.

"We wear the feathers, fur, and hair. We know where the shell is. We have the water from the Dragon World," I said. "All we need is something to warm the potion. Eldest Great Dragon said it must be warm—not hot—so Nah'ee can drink it."

Kisin ordered two men to fetch wood for a fire. He motioned for Bruyah and the guard to go for the Sacred Stone pieces and another man to return to the village for a kettle to heat the potion.

Nah'ee slept on with Yochi, Tahli, and Arald humming to keep her calm. No nightmares. No Terror.

There wasn't much for Oma and me to do, so we shared Dragon beans while we waited.

Chapter Nineteen—Dragon Water

I was really ready to get some sleep and Arald was already in my pack, snoring, when Bruyah came into the clearing with a heavy sack. She spread the pieces of shell on a cloth in front of Kisin. "The Sacred Stone broke into only a few pieces," she said, fingering one of the smaller curved chunks.

The shell really did look like stone. I picked up a piece, ignoring Bruyah's glare. The shell was heavy like stone, too. The whole thing would have been about the size of a lopsided basketball. Big for an egg, but much too small to hold Nah'ee now. She had grown a lot in less than two weeks.

"We'd better get this potion ready soon," I said to Oma. "I'm not sure what it will do, but if we have to carry her to the Black Line Rock, we don't want her growing much more!"

"What do we do with the shell?" Kisin asked.

"We have to make the pieces small enough to mix with the Dragon World water so Nah'ee can drink the potion," I explained. I looked at Oma. "Last time, the dragons ground the rock for us. How do we do it this time?"

Oma picked up a shell piece. "This may feel like stone, Benjamin, but it isn't really." She held it so I could see the broken edge. "See? It's not solid. It's honeycombed like the inside of a bone."

"The pieces can be broken up?" Bruyah said.

Bruyah brought over a rock the size of a fist. I put a piece of the shell on top of the sack. BAM! Bruyah slammed the rock onto the shell. At first it looked like nothing had happened. Then the piece simply collapsed into small shards.

Bruyah grinned and snatched another piece of shell. Soon we were both banging rocks on the shell pieces. The pile of large egg shells became a pile of pieces that were almost like dust.

"Now we heat the Dragon World water and put in the shell pieces." Kisin said. The men had already set up the fire with a tripod over it to hold the kettle. But nobody was able to lift the log bucket because I had to be touching it.

I sighed. It had wanted me to carry it, then to keep my hand on it while the mule carried it. Now it seemed to want me to carry it again. Arald said silently, *"Benmin must take bucket."*

And Tahli said at the same time, *"Must pour Dragon World water into kettle. Then the shell."*

I went over and picked up the bucket. The heavy log bucket. My arms did *not* want to do this. "What dragons decree shall certainly be," I said, gritting my teeth. "Some dragon power would be nice."

"Benjamin," Oma cautioned.

"I know. I know. Dragon power is for emergencies only." I hauled the bucket to the kettle. I'd never be able to lift it high enough to pour the water into the kettle, I thought. Then Kisin was beside me. He put one hand under the bottom of the bucket, braced himself against the tripod and together we heaved the lip of the bucket over the edge of the kettle. Kisin held the kettle steady and Oma helped me tip the bucket.

Dragon World water isn't like regular water. It's really thick. No wonder it didn't splash out on the trip here. Even tipping the bucket more only made the water slowly ooze into the kettle. Slowly, like pouring molasses that's been in the refrigerator, the bucket emptied and the kettle filled.

"I remember reading about heavy water in my history books," I said out loud. "It was used to make bombs, but it also has good uses. I wonder if this is like that."

Oma shook her head. "I don't think Dragon World water is the same. But one good use of this heavy water is to get Nah'ee to the Dragon World."

We all stood around watching as the thick water warmed over the fire. Kisin and Oma gathered the shell dust in the middle of the cloth. "When do we mix this with the water?" Oma asked.

"The Eldest Great Dragon didn't say when to do that. Just that the Power parts of three dragons and three dragon-bound in this world have to be put in all at the same time."

Just then Nah'ee woke up. Hungry. The men were sent for more of the grey-green leaves she liked. Yochi and Tahli began humming. Kisin fed her as fast as the men brought the leaves. That left Oma, Arald, me, and Bruyah to watch the water.

"Girl still thinks wrong," Arald said silently. *"Thinks she, Nah'ee be dragon-bound."*

"Well, she won't be," I thought to him firmly. "That can't happen. Great Dragons don't partner with humans."

Oma put her hand on the side of the kettle. "Almost body temperature," she said. "That's right for human babies." She turned to Kisin. "Is Nah'ee warmer than a human?"

Kisin held his hand against the hatchling's stomach. "Some warmer than my hand."

"Well, we don't want to make this drink too hot for her," Oma said, touching the kettle again.

"Metal holds heat, so maybe if we took it off the fire now, it should stay warm enough," I suggested.

Oma motioned two of the men to lift the kettle off the fire. They laid it on a flat spot in the center of the clearing.

The dragons kept humming. Arald nodded. *"Put shells in first, then others?"* he asked, silently, still humming.

"I think that should work," I answered without speaking. Then out loud I said, "Put the shells in, then maybe we all stand around the kettle and drop in our parts at the same time?" I sort of asked the others.

Kisin stood up. Nah'ee nudged him for more food. Bruyah took over the feeding and Kisin joined us.

"We must have First Mother ceremony," he said firmly. "First Mother must know we follow what must be done."

"The water's already warm," I said silently. "We can't let it get cool again."

Tahli stopped humming and nodded toward Oma. She nodded back. "We have time for a *short* ceremony," she told Kisin.

He told the men to prepare a small circle around the kettle. They drew the lines marking off quadrants. "Place the stool here," Kisin told them, pointing to a spot not far from the kettle. "The kettle will be the center. Nah'ee will be in the south quadrant."

We all went to where Kisin pointed. Oma and Tahli in one quadrant, Arald and I in the opposite one. Kisin and Yochi stood across from Bruyah and Nah'ee. Bruyah stood proudly, still feeding Nah'ee.

"Girl thinks she is dragon-bound now," Arald told me. *"Not. We would know?"* he sort of asked.

"She is balancing Kisin and Yochi who are dragon-bound." I thought slowly. "Maybe they are bound together in a different way." I sighed and shook my head. "Maybe. 'What dragons decree shall certainly be.' So maybe anything is possible."

"*How? Nah'ee in Dragon World. Girl here,*" Arald looked puzzled.

"I don't know." I shook my head and stroked his belly as he stood on my shoulder.

Chapter Twenty—The Potion

Kisin raised his staff. The forest became silent. No bird sounded. No wind moved the leaves. Nothing. I could hear my heart beating. He swung his staff so the other end was down and made four holes in the dirt—one in each quadrant. He took some flowers from a small pile at his feet. He gently picked out the stamens filled with pollen and dropped them in the first hole.

The petals went into the second hole. A couple of the grey-green leaves were buried next. In the last hole, Kisin placed a small pinch of the shell dust. When it was covered, he stood and moved to the stool. He lifted the cloth that had covered the stool, sat down, and draped the cloth over his head.

Kisin raised the cloth and looked up at the sky. "First Mother, Aluna, we ask your help," he said in a slow, deep voice. "We prepare a potion that will help the Great Child of Quetzalcoatl get home. We seek your guidance in this. We are balanced. Old balances young. Know more balances know less. Above is sky. Below is earth. All is balanced. First Mother, Aluna, guide us to do right."

The jungle sounds came back. We could now do what had to be done. Oma felt the kettle again. "Still warm," she said, smiling.

Nah'ee was drooping. She was tired again. The dragons hummed her to sleep while the rest of us prepared to make the potion. "How do we get a sleeping Great Dragon baby to drink the potion when it is ready," I wondered.

"Nah'ee will not sleep long. We must have the potion ready for her. She will be thirsty then." Kisin said.

The Dragon World water was the right temperature. We had the crushed shell. And the feathers, fur, and hair were right here. I drew in a long breath and nodded. Oma nodded. Kisin did, too. The men drew away from the center of the circle. Bruyah stayed beside Nah'ee, ready to feed her leaves if she woke up. The dragons all perched on nearby branches and peered into the kettle.

"Do we all have to put the shell into the water together?" Oma asked me.

I frowned, thinking. I had to remember this right. There wouldn't be a second chance. "We need three threes to make the potion," I said, starting at the beginning. "Three dragons, three humans dragon-bound. And the potion which needs part of Nah'ee past, part of Nah'ee present, and part of Nah'ee future."

"This we know," Yochi said, shaking his wings.

"Nah'ee past is her shell," I said, ignoring Yochi. "Nah'ee present is from three dragons—Yochi, Tahli, and Arald—and from three dragon-bound humans—Oma, Kisin, and me. Nah'ee future is Dragon World water." Going over directions more than once helped me remember. "Eldest Great Dragon said we MUST put the hair, feathers, and fur in at the same time, but separate." I thought again. "She didn't say the shell had to be put in any special way, so I guess that really doesn't matter."

"Good," Kisin said. "I will pour the shell powder into the Dragon World water. Then we all must take from our bodies what was stated. Together we drop those into the mix. What happens then?"

I shrugged and looked at Arald. He cocked his head, 'talking' to Tahli. She dipped her head down, then up. Undecided.

"Let me put the shell powder in," Bruyah said. "I am to be dragon-bound to Nah'ee, so I should be included."

Kisin looked shocked. "The Eldest Great Dragon lives in a different world. You cannot be bound to her and be Manos here."

Arald and I looked at each other. We nodded.

Bruyah stood straight. "The prophecy says that the Child and Mamos-to-be will learn together to live. We will bring balance again to the world. This world." She said, her head tilted back and staring at Kisin like he was not important. "Nah'ee is the Child. I am Mamos-to-be. We will balance the world, which *you* haven't done."

Kisin pounded his staff on the ground once, twice, three times. Then with the final BAM, he pointed the top of the staff directly at Bruyah. "Patience you do not have yet. Mamos must have patience. You are not yet Mamos," he said, his face looking like one of those wooden voodoo masks I'd seen in a museum. Really scary.

Bruyah slunk back a few steps. She bowed her head and seemed almost as small as Nah'ee.

"She feels shame," Arald said. *"Should."*

"Yeah," I told him silently. "But the prophecy does say they'll learn to live together."

Tahli heard us and said out loud, *"They learn 'together to live.' Not live together dragon-bound."*

"We shall soon find out," Oma said, gathering up the cloth that had the shell powder. She handed it to Kisin and waved him toward the kettle.

He stepped closer to the kettle, looked in at the slowly roiling thick water, and swallowed. Very carefully, he tipped the bag over the rim of the kettle and into the water. He jumped back. I think we were all expecting some kind of reaction, but nothing happened. We all looked back into the kettle. There was a whitish powder covering the surface of the water.

"Should we mix it in?" I asked anyone.

"Did the Eldest Great Dragon say anything about stirring?" Oma asked me.

I thought. "Actually, she had Taranoka tell us the directions. But no, he didn't say anything about mixing. Just put in the shell, put in the hair and stuff for Power. The only MUST was that we all do that last part together."

"Then no stirring," Kisin said firmly.

Ben and Arald and The Lost Baby

The three of us took our places around the kettle. The dragons landed on our shoulders. "Wait," I said. "We have to have the feathers, fur, and hair ready to drop in at the same time."

We all stepped back a bit. Oma reached up to her coil of hair, slid a finger close to her scalp, wrapped one strand around her finger, and yanked. A long, orangy, slightly curled hair slowly came loose, slipping from one round coil to the other until she held a strand of hair that was nearly as long as she is tall.

Kisin was next. His hair was not as long, but it was gathered in a knot at the back of his head. His straight black hair got tangled a bit, but he managed to pull it loose.

Then it was my turn. My kind-of brown hair is short, so it didn't take me long to jerk a piece from the top of my head.

We all looked at the dragons. Arald used his claw to pull out a small clump of red-gold fur. Tahli did the same with her own brassy-gold fur. Tochi stood tall. *"Feathers better than fur,"* he exclaimed as he easily pulled one of the fluffy, iridescent feathers from his belly. Everyone, even Kisin, ignored him.

"Now we stand equal around the kettle," Kisin said, looking around at us. "I will say GO and we drop our parts at the same time."

Oma shook her head. "It will be better to count down from three."

Kisin nodded. "Great Dragons like threes," he said, dipping his head to me.

Nervously, I took one step closer to the kettle. I could see Oma doing the same, then Kisin stepped up with his hair in his hand. Together three dragons and three dragon-bound humans held out the required Power parts.

"Three." Kisin stood straighter and tossed a glance upwards. "Aluna help us. Two. One"

Hair, fur, and feathers drifted from our hands onto the surface of the Dragon World water. Then…nothing.

We all looked at each other.

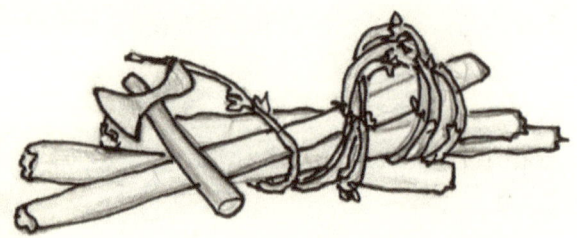

Chapter Twenty-One—A Stone Dragon

Suddenly, there was a *hiss, HISS*, then a much louder *HISS*. The Dragon World water started to foam. The shell powder and the hair, fur, and feathers disappeared into the foaming water. *HISS. HISS. HISS.* Then a third set: *HISS, HISS, hiss.*

"Well, Great Dragons really do like threes," I said, still looking into the kettle. The water was no longer so thick. It had a color to it, too. But like colors in the Dragon World, this wasn't any color I'd seen before.

A cloud of steam poured over the rim and drifted toward Bruyah and Nah'ee. Nah'ee lifted her head and sniffed. She lunged toward the kettle. Her long neck leaned over the edge. A long tongue dipped into the potion. She blinked. And blinked again. With a final blink, she shoved her head into the kettle and slurped noisily.

We all sighed. Nah'ee was drinking the potion.

"Now what?" Kisin asked. We all shrugged, even Yochi.

The directions had only told us how to make the potion and for Nah'ee to drink, not what to do then. I had guessed that it would put her to sleep so we could carry her to the Black Line Rock and then to Hidden Valley and the portal.

We waited and listened as Nah'ee finished the potion, sliding her tongue around the bottom to get every drop. We watched as she drooped until her belly was on the ground, her tail curled around her, and her head rested on her feet. She blinked a few times, then stopped moving.

No twitch of skin or flicker of an eyelid. Nothing. She wasn't just not moving, she wasn't breathing! Bruyah touched Nah'ee. "She's hard!" she cried. "Like stone." Bruyah turned and lunged toward me, her hands out like claws. "You! You have killed Nah'ee! You will pay!"

Arald flew off my shoulder, leaving claw marks on the pad. His eyes were red swirls and his claws were extended. "Arald!" I yelled and reached for him. "No!"

Kisin reached to grab Bruyah, but missed. Oma was closer. She took one step forward. "NO!" she shouted at Bruyah. She put her hands on Bruyah's shoulders. "No," she said more softly.

"The Eldest Great Dragon would not put her child in danger." Oma looked at me and nodded.

"Tell her," Tahli said to me silently.

"Tell her? Tell her what?" I thought back, still worried about Arald. I know he wanted to defend me, but this wasn't the time.

Arald flew in circles around us. *"Tell what potion do,"* Arald said. His eyes were still mostly red, but his words had purple tinges that told me he wasn't sure what to do, either.

I stepped back far enough to be out of Bruyah's reach. "The Eldest Great Dragon wants Nah'ee in the Dragon World with her." I told her. That I was sure of. Arald agreed.

"You lie!" Bruyah tried to escape Oma's grip. "You want only to keep me from being dragon-bound to Nah'ee!"

I shook my head. "The potion was so we could take her down the mountain to the Black Line Rock."

Kisin's head jerked up. Now Yochi's eyes swirled red and purple. "The Black Line is known only to Kocqui," Kisin said. "You know of this?"

"Arald and I found a rock lying on the Black Line. The rock had a shell and spider carved on it. We touched it and we were back home in Hidden Valley."

"We come back same way," Arald said, finally settling on my shoulder again. He stood tall and stared angrily at Bruyah. His eyes were still a mix of red and purple, but some blue was there now, too.

Kisin bowed his head, then looked at Bruyah. "They do not lie, Bruyah. They have seen the Black Line and the Rock of the First Mother."

Bruyah blinked back tears. Oma pushed on Bruyah's shoulders until she sat on the ground in front of the stone-like Nah'ee. "The prophecy said we are to learn together to live," Bruyah said sadly. "How can we live if one is stone?"

"Nah'ee won't always be stone," I said. I *almost* felt sorry for her. "The potion worked. Nah'ee wouldn't leave the portal without it. Now she can be carried to the Black Line Rock."

Oma nodded. "We don't know how long the potion will last. It would be best if we did not waste time."

Kisin stood tall, still staring at Bruyah with his eyes nearly shut. "You have not patience nor wisdom yet to be Mamos. You will help carry Nah'ee," he ordered. Bruyah just looked at Nah'ee. She had been so sure they would be dragon-bound by now.

I tried to figure out how much a stone dragon would weigh. More than a log bucket of Dragon World water, I guessed. "How will we carry her down the mountain?" I asked Oma.

Kisin answered. "This we know." He spoke to the men with the machetes. They trotted off into the jungle. The guards followed. "They bring what is needed."

Tahli landed on Oma's shoulder, chittering. Oma nodded. "We should begin the journey at first light. We must get Nah'ee to the Black Line Rock, then from the center of Hidden Valley to the portal in the cliff there. That will take several hours. Can all be ready by first light?" she asked Kisin.

He looked up at the sky. "The dark is nearly half over," he said. "There is much yet to do. The men and I go only as far as the Black Line. We will prepare what must be done to carry Quetzalcoatl's Child home."

The men came back carrying long poles and vines. "These men and Bruyah and I will work. Ancient Mother," he said, bowing toward Oma, "and young partner of Quetzal Child," he added, bowing toward me, "must rest. The Quetzal Children can also rest."

I didn't expect to be able to get to sleep even though I was about as tired as I'd ever been. But I curled up in one of the Kocqui blankets with my pack as a pillow. Arald scrabbled around a bit getting comfortable. He tucked his head under one wing. Even before he started to snore, I was asleep. The last thing I remember seeing was Oma leaning back against a tree trunk as if she was in her rocking chair.

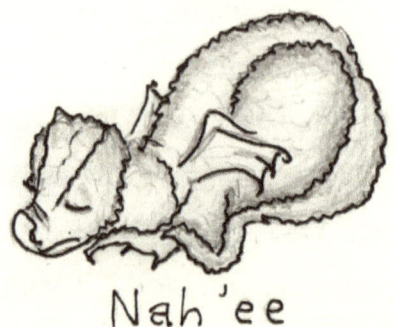

Nah'ee

Chapter Twenty-Two—Heading Home

The smell of coffee woke me up. It was still dark. Oma was at the fire, pouring the thickest coffee I'd ever seen into a cup made from some kind of leaf twisted into a cone shape. She handed it to me, but one whiff and I knew I'd rather drink some of the Nah'ee potion than that. Oma smiled. "It's not that bad, Benjamin. They thicken it with some sap that takes the bitterness away. Try it," she ordered, pushing the cup at me.

I sighed, but followed orders. It was only polite. I touched the liquid with my tongue, expecting to have to gag. But it wasn't bad. Not good, but not bad. "Well, the Dragon beans are better, but this isn't too bad," I told her.

Arald woke up. *"Bacon?"* he asked, yawning.

"No bacon. Coffee and…" I looked at the food lying on another, very big leaf. "Looks like some of those not-quite tortillas and a kind of mush."

Arald took a piece of the not-quite tortilla. *"Like mountain food place,"* he said, then gulped down some of the nearly solid coffee. *"Good mush,"* he added, wiping his claws on the log.

I grinned. "That was the coffee," I told him. "The mush is in the leaf bowl there," I added, pointing to a leaf curled into a bowl that held some greenish pasty stuff.

"Hmmph." Arald dipped a claw into the mush and tasted it. *"Mush fuzzy. Coffee better."*

Fuzzy mush? I dipped a finger into the bowl. It was fizzy. And tasted a bit like caramel—with fizz. "You take the coffee," I told him. "I'll eat the fizzy mush."

Finally, I was awake enough to be interested in what was going on around me. The men and Kisin and Bruyah had created a cage-like box with poles running through it so it could be carried by a couple of men. Now they were trying to put Nah'ee into the box. I was right. She was heavy.

The men didn't really want to touch Nah'ee. Or maybe she didn't want them to touch her. Either way, *they* couldn't move her. So Oma, Bruyah, Kisin, and I had to lift her enough to let the men slide the bottom of the box under her. They tied the bottom to the rest of the box and put the long poles through. With two men holding the poles in front and two in the back, they were able to lift Nah'ee with only a few grunts.

The sky was showing through the trees when we set off down the mountain. The four men were strong, but as strong as they were, it wasn't an easy job. The trail was rocky and crooked and narrow. The rest of us couldn't help. The dragons made sure animals kept their distance, so we didn't need the guards. That was good because the guards were helping to carry Nah'ee.

"Hungry," Arald grumbled. *"Coffee food not enough."*

"I'm hungry, too," I told him. "But we have to get Nah'ee home before that potion wears off."

Tahli must have heard us. Oma came up beside me and asked very quietly, "Are you sure the potion wears off? Or must we do something to return Nah'ee to life?"

Oh, boy! I hadn't thought about that. I bit my bottom lip. "The Great Dragons didn't say anything about undoing the potion," I whispered back.

"Eldest Great Dragon say bring Nah'ee to Dragon World," Arald said silently.

"Yes," I told Oma. "Eldest Great Dragon just said to bring Nah'ee from the Black Line Rock to Qua-na-tse-ne, then through the portal."

"Then that is what we do," Oma said in a normal voice. "What dragons decree, shall certainly be."

"I do wish what dragons decree would be a little bit clearer, though," I thought to Arald.

He and Tahli both nodded. Oma raised an eyebrow, but didn't say anything.

"Still hungry," Arald complained.

I fished out one of the Dragon beans and gave it to him. "That will have to hold you for a while," I said.

First light was long past by the time we got to the pillars that marked the end of Kocqui territory. The men put the box down. They looked to Kisin. He looked at me. "Where is the Black Line Rock?" he asked like a teacher testing a student.

I looked at the ground between the pillars. At first, I couldn't see anything but dirt. Then I noticed a faint black line. It grew darker and wider as I looked. It went under one pillar and continued into the jungle. "Here," I said, pointing to the line and then to the jungle. "It goes that way."

Kisin knelt down. He reached out as though to touch the line. "The Black Line is *here*." He beckoned to Bruyah. She knelt beside him. "Look. See the Line?" Kisin asked her.

Bruyah leaned forward, looking closely at the dirt in front of her. Then she jerked back. "A line!" she said loudly. "There really *is* a Black Line." She leaned back on her heels and looked up at me. "You are not Kocqui, but you see the Black Line clearly. I am Kocqui and I see only faintly." She looked back at the box that held Nah'ee. "I am not worthy," she said sadly.

Oma touched Bruyah's shoulder. "We each do what is meant for us," she said. "It is for Benjamin and Arald to follow the Black Line to the Rock that will take us to Hidden Valley. It is for us to follow them." She smiled at me.

Kisin motioned the men to pick up the box and to follow Arald and me into the jungle.

I swallowed hard. What if we couldn't find the Rock again?

"We find," Arald said with bright blue spots. *"Dragons decree."*

"I sure hope so." I stepped out, my eyes on the ground so I didn't lose the Black Line. We didn't have to go far. Only a hundred steps or so and there it was. The Black Line Rock. The shell and spider carvings glowed blue against the black earth. "Here," I called back to the others.

Kisin came up beside me. He gasped. "Never have I seen the First Mother so bright. Truly, this is what must be."

The men lowered the box with Nah'ee in it so it touched the Black Line Rock. They stepped back quickly. Kisin, too, stepped back, pulling Bruyah with him. "This is for the Ancient Mother, the Young Dragon-bound and the furred Quetzal Children to do now." He bowed deeply toward us and motioned the men to leave. They, too, bowed, then wasted no time getting away from the magic rock that glowed blue.

Arald leaned against me as I knelt beside the Black Line Rock. Tahli was on Oma's shoulder and Oma put one hand on my shoulder and the other on the box with Nah'ee. I reached out to the Rock. I had to make sure we were all touching before I made contact with the Rock.

I didn't notice Bruyah pulling from Kisin's grasp and lunging toward us. Suddenly, her foot came down on top of my hands. That pushed my palms flat, forcing them against the Black Line Rock.

Gorse   Bracken

Chapter Twenty-Three—Hidden Valley

I tried to pull my hands back, but we had already disappeared from Colombia. We were kneeling next to Qua-nya-tse-né in Hidden Valley.

Bruyah fell back. She was sitting on the ground, scrambling to get away from us. "Th-the p-prophecy said Nah'ee and I w-will l-learn together to live," she stammered with a scared look on her face. "You said it is for *us* to follow them," she added, looking at Oma defiantly.

Tahli skreeled, flying off Oma's shoulder and heading toward Bruyah.

Arald's eyes were bright red swirls. *"Girl go back"* he bellowed. His wings beat at my head. I leaned away and fell sideways. One hand landed in the shallows of Long Creek. I grabbed at the box that held Nah'ee. Somehow, I managed to stay more or less upright, though the box did tilt farther into the water.

Only Oma stayed on her feet. She waved Tahli back. "No, Tahli," Oma spoke calmly. "What is done is done. What dragons decree shall certainly be," she said, squeezing my shoulder.

"You think they meant Bruyah to come with us?" I asked, getting to my feet. "Why couldn't they tell us?" I was angry. The dragons told Arald and me to bring Nah'ee home, but they wouldn't tell us about Bruyah?

"Girl go Dragon World?" Arald asked, red showing his anger with purple that meant he didn't understand.

"I don't understand, either," I told him. "I don't know *anything*," I added, disgusted with Eldest Great Dragon and her secrets.

Bruyah just sat there, a stunned look on her face. She wasn't the proud, better-than-everyone girl I knew in Colombia. She didn't seem to really know why she was here.

Tahli and Arald fluttered around the girl, skreeling. They were still angry and confused. So was I. Oma helped me to my feet, then stepped toward Bruyah. Bruyah shrank back. "I am to be with Nah'ee," she said in a quivery voice, holding her hands out.

Oma shook out her skirts. "Benjamin, is Nah'ee as she was?" she asked me, still looking at Bruyah.

I looked at the box. A couple of the slats had cracked. I put my hand through and touched Nah'ee. Hard. Like stone. "She's the same. Looks like she isn't changing back here."

"We'd best hurry, then," Oma said, her eyes never leaving Bruyah. "While it is still morning, it will take us hours to get to the portal with only three to carry the box. And we must repair the box before we carry it. Full dark comes quickly once the sun leaves the Valley."

I looked past her. I blinked. "Uh, Oma?" I said, not sure I'd really seen what I thought I'd seen. "Oma?"

"You have an idea how we can transport the box, Benjamin?" Oma asked.

"I think so." I pointed. Bruyah turned first. Oma lifted her head and looked beyond the girl. The dragons were still flitting and skreeling angrily.

Oma smiled. "Bracken. Of course."

I *had* seen a mule, then. Bracken who came when needed. He hadn't come when I was carrying the heavy log bucket, but he was here now, munching on grass and waiting to be noticed. And he wasn't alone. Another mule was beside him just as contentedly having a grass snack.

"Ah," Oma said, walking past Bruyah and the still skreeling dragons. "I believe your name is Gorse." She reached out and the female mule nuzzled her hand.

"Arald! Tahli!" I called. "Stop that fussing and come here!" I ordered.

"Girl bad," Arald answered, still flying around. Tahli just kept flying closer and closer to Bruyah's head.

"Arald!" I called again. "Look at Oma," I said, pointing. "Tahli! Look at Oma!" I called again. I started walking toward Oma and the mules.

Finally, Tahli turned and saw Oma. She gave one more skreel and flew to Oma's shoulder. Arald plopped down on my shoulder, his claws still fully out. "Ouch. Watch it, Arald. That hurts."

Arald dipped his head a bit. *"Sorry. Angry."*

"Yeah. I noticed." I said, rubbing where his claws had dug in. "We need to get Nah'ee to the portal. And the dragons have given us the way to do it."

"We must hurry," Oma said. "Bracken, you stand here and Gorse, you go beside him." The mules did as she asked. "Benjamin. Bruyah. We must lift the box by the poles and tie them to the mules. They will take Nah'ee across the Valley and up the cliffside to the portal."

Bruyah and I went back to where we had landed. The box was tilted with one end nearly in Long Creek. I waded into the water and lifted that end. Well, I tried to lift it. Bruyah came to help, but even together, we couldn't move it.

That's when we heard someone coming toward us along the trail from Oma's house. Then a deep voice called. "Oma? Ben? Is that you?"

That was Dad's voice. "Dad?" I called at the same time Oma said, "James. You come at a good time."

Dad appeared carrying a coil of rope and a pack. "Dad!" I stepped from the water, slid on one knee, then made it to my feet. "Dad! What are you doing here?" I asked him.

He smiled. "We suddenly thought it would be a good idea to come. I wasn't sure why until I heard the dragons skreeling.

Ben and Arald and The Lost Baby   Karel Henneberger

Looks like you've brought some visitors," he said, looking at Bruyah and the box with Nah'ee.

I looked at him. Then, slowly I said, "What dragons decree..."

"...shall certainly be," he finished, nodding solemnly.

"Dragon power works when needed," Oma said. "We'll explain as we work," she added. "We must repair the broken slats on the box first."

Dad slipped off his pack, dug around in it a bit and came out with a roll of duct tape. "A couple of sticks for braces and some tape and the box should be ready to go."

It took a bit longer than he expected, thanks to having to get the box out of the stream first, then finding the right sticks.

Oma pulled two blankets from Dad's pack. She laid one over Bracken's back and the other over Gorse's. "Now. Lift the box by the poles." She directed Bruyah and me to take the upper ends. Oma and Dad stooped and lifted the lower poles. Dad and Oma were strong enough, but it was really hard for Bruyah and me to lift our end. We finally just twisted the box around so the mules could stand with the box between them.

"Oma," Dad said, reaching into his pack. "I brought some sandwiches and chips. I thought Ben and Arald might be hungry." He grinned. "Better eat before we head out."

"Arald hungry," he said, settling on top of the box.

"Arald! Not on top of Nah'ee," I said.

"Not hurt Nah'ee. Feed Arald." One claw reached out and took one of the sandwiches. *"Bacon. Good. Better even than Dragon beans."*

Dad held a sandwich out to me, then offered Bruyah one. She looked scared. "Oh, Dad. This is Bruyah. She wasn't supposed to come here." I stopped. "I don't *think* she was, anyway."

"Well, hello, Bruyah," Dad said, still holding a sandwich out toward her. "I hope you like bacon sandwiches."

"Tahli," Oma said sternly. "Translate for James, please." Apparently, Oma and I had need to understand Kisin and Bruyah and the others, but Dad didn't.

Tahli tossed her head. Her eyes were still swirling red slightly, but she chittered and Bruyah could understand what Dad said now. She gave a small smile and hesitantly took the sandwich. Biting into it, she grinned. "Baygan sanches."

Dad smiled. "Oma?"

Oma sighed. "Very well, James, since you brought them along." Her sandwich was gone before mine was barely half eaten. Of course, Arald was already on his second one. Tahli was neatly dissecting a small piece of Oma's.

Oma brushed crumbs from her skirts and slapped her hands together. "Now," she said. "We have enough time, but it will be slow going. We must first get the box with Nah'ee tied to the mules so we can get moving."

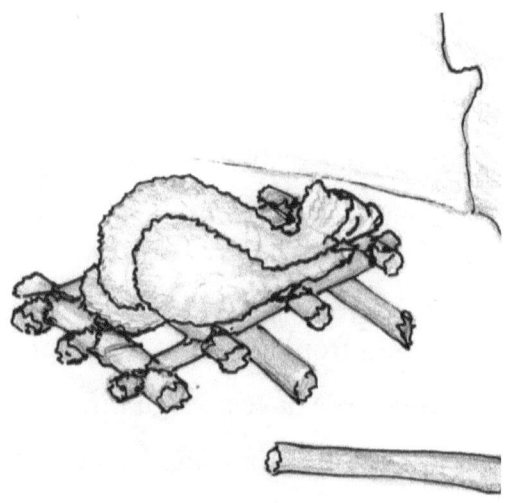

Chapter Twenty-Four—To the Portal

Dad tied two pieces of rope around Bracken's belly. He made a small loop on the top just behind Bracken's neck and another right over his rump. Then he did the same with Gorse. With Dad's help, we were able to lift the box so the poles could slide into the loops he'd made.

Slowly, Bracken and Gorse stepped out together. It took a long time and the sun was pretty far into evening when we reached the beginning of the path up the cliffside. Dad reached into his pack again and pulled out some flashlights. At least, they looked like flashlights. But I knew from sad experience that batteries don't work in Hidden Valley. No electric stuff does. I looked at Dad. "For some reason, I thought they might be a good idea," he said.

"They will work if they are needed," Oma said, taking one and turning the switch. Light. Bright light.

"I guess they are needed," I said, taking one from Dad.

Dad grinned. "What dragons decree…" He turned the last flashlight on and moved to the back of our convoy.

I grinned back. "…shall certainly be."

Oma just shook her head at us and led the mules along the path up to the portal. They stepped in perfect unison. The box with Nah'ee barely wobbled at all.

The trip was a lot easier with the mules carrying the heavy box. It was still slow going, though. The path seemed a bit wider, but even more twisty and rocky than when I was carrying the log bucket of Dragon World water. Maybe dragon power had helped me then.

"Not dragons," Arald said. He hesitated. Then, *"Maybe."*

Tahli chittered. Oma looked back at me. "Humans have powers, too, Benjamin. Not like dragon powers. Ours work in different ways."

I thought of Oma going *through* doors and moving things without touching them. If those were human powers, I hoped I'd learn them, too.

"Can," Arald said silently. *"When older?"* he said with small blue splotches and larger purple ones flickering in my head.

"So we have to learn more about a lot of things?" I asked him.

He nodded and fluffed out his wings. *"We grow. We learn."*

Then we were standing in front of the rock that just looked like the rest of the cliff except for a faint zig-zag mark. But all of us except Bruyah knew it hid the portal to the Dragon World. We were there, but how were we to get Nah'ee through? I looked at Dad. He looked at Oma.

"Well," she finally said. "Bracken and Gorse certainly can't go through. Neither can I or James. And the box is too big."

"Take the box apart first, then," Dad said, looking over the construction.

So we did. First, we slid the poles from the loops in the rope around Bracken, then did the same with Gorse. Dad untied the ropes around their bellies. The mules shook a few times.

Bracken snorted. Gorse dipped her head and they headed back down the trail to wherever they stay when they aren't needed.

"There is a farmer nearby who lets them use his barn," Oma said when she saw me looking after them. Of course. The mules come when needed and a farmer lets them stay when they're not. Naturally.

Dad untied the lashings on the box and lifted the top part off. Nah'ee was still hard like stone. "Now what?" Dad asked.

I looked at the zig-zaggy place on the cliffside where I knew the portal was. I remembered how we'd gotten Nah'ee into the box in the first place. "Back in Colombia, the men couldn't touch Nah'ee. Kisin, Oma, Bruyah and I lifted her so the men could slide the bottom of the box under her." I looked at Nah'ee lying there like a statue and remembered how heavy she had been to lift with four people.

"Four here," Arald said silently with just a hint of purple. *"You. Oma. Girl. Dad."*

"Yeah, but can Dad do it?" I said out loud.

"Do what, son?" he asked me.

"Will the dragons decree that you help us lift Nah'ee. It took four of us to get her into the box. And the Kocqui men couldn't touch Nah'ee at all."

Oma nodded. "Bracken and Gorse were called for a reason. Their reason is over. They have left. James was called for a reason. He is still here."

We learned something in school about logical thinking. Oma's argument seemed logical in a Dragon World kind of way. "So the four of us get Nah'ee as close to the portal as we can. Then what? Shove her through?"

"Let's get the 'to the portal' part finished first," Dad said. He and Oma looked at the box, then at Nah'ee, then at the portal. "Maybe slide the box closer to the cliff?" Dad asked, absently rolling one of the poles between his hands

"Wait." I sat on my heels and thought. Something about rolling sticks under things. I looked at Dad. "Rolling sticks? Put some pieces of the poles under the box like they did on Easter Island to move those statues?"

Dad clapped his hand on my back. "Good thinking, Ben. It worked for much heavier things in the past. Should work here now."

It wasn't quite that easy, though. First Dad and I used our knives to cut the poles into short enough pieces to fit through the narrow portal. That took a while. An axe would have come in handy, I thought to myself. Then I shook my head. The dragons had made sure we had what we needed. No more. No less.

I was glad the dragons had decreed we needed light. With Oma, Dad, and Bruyah lifting one end of the box, I slid a piece of pole under as far as I could, then another closer to the edge. The three lifted the other end and I put another piece underneath the box.

They put the weight down on the pole pieces and the box moved! Bruyah shouted and clapped her hands.

"Wait," Dad said. "We need to keep rollers ahead of where we are going. Ben, push another one right at the front edge."

We only needed to move it a few feet. With the rollers, it took only four easy shoves to get the box right up next to the cliff.

Tahli walked into the portal. Arald fluttered above me. Bruyah and I pushed Nah'ee over the last of the rollers into the tunnel that led to the Dragon World. We were all in the darkness that was the portal. Bruyah grabbed my arm. She yelled something that wasn't translated.

I remembered the first time I'd gone through and grinned. I pried her hand off my arm. "Look ahead," I told her. "That's the Dragon World."

As I said that, we were standing on the ledge. Hundreds of dragons and wyverns crowded the valley beneath us. All were quiet. None grumbled or snorted fire.

"You are well come, friends." The old-fashioned English told me who had spoken.

I turned. "The Old—Kembe," I said. I'd almost called him the Old Man. "And Polter. Good to see you."

Kembe bowed. "You have done well, Tahli, Arald, and young Benjamin."

I could see Bruyah standing still, pressed against the cliff. Her eyes were wide open and she was shaking as if there was a strong wind. I sighed. I didn't like her, but I knew what it's like to be scared senseless. I reached out and pulled her arm. "Welcome to the Dragon World," I said with just a tiny bit of pleasure at seeing her so frightened.

Arose arrived with Chobah not far behind. Kembe and Polter would go with Chobah. Bruyah and I and the small dragons would fit on Arose. But how to get Nah'ee on?

"Penmose arrives. Penmose will carry Eldest Great Dragon's Baby to her," Arose said in his gravelly voice.

With Bruyah behind me and Tahli and Arald riding on his head, Arose lifted above the ledge. Kembe and Polter climbed on Chobah who took a position nearby. Suddenly, a larger dragon hovered near the ledge. It was the third Great Dragon of the Council. The one that never said anything.

He carefully curled his claws around the statue-like body of Nah'ee, cradling her in a basket of dragon claws. Slowly, Penmose rose and, with a gentle flap of his wings, lifted into the air. With great ceremony, he flew across the Dragon World valley. Arose and Chobah followed, one on each side of Penmose and slightly behind.

Long necked dragons, short stubby ones, and everything in between craned to see the Eldest Great Dragon's Lost Baby. Bruyah squeezed my waist hard. She had her head tucked into my back. I was sure her eyes were shut tight.

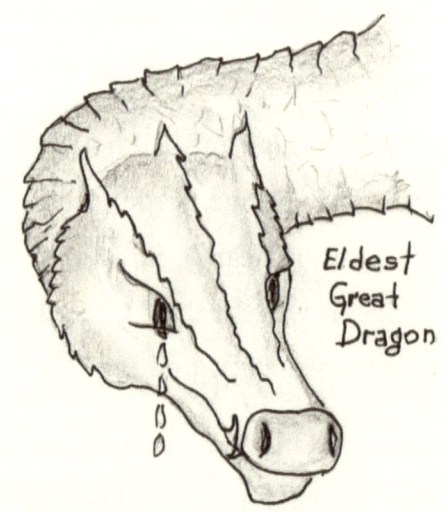

Eldest
Great
Dragon

Chapter Twenty-Five—Reunion

The trip took longer than it ever had before, but when we got to the ledge where the Great Dragon Council met, there was only the Eldest Great Dragon. Penmose hovered above the ledge, gently opened his claws and set Nah'ee down in front of her mother. He flew to a flat spot nearby.

Arose and Chobah came close enough to the ledge for us to climb off, then they, too flew to sit by Penmose. We stood still, watching Eldest Great Dragon. Her eyes swirled with more colors than I had names for, but red wasn't one of them. That was a good sign.

She bent her head, touching Nah'ee with her nose. She sniffed. Two large tears slipped down her long snout and landed on the head of her Lost Baby. Nothing seemed to happen. Then I saw a dot of color appear on the top of Nah'ee's head. Then another.

Two more tears plopped onto Nah'ee. More and more colored scales appeared. Whatever was in those tears was dissolving the stone-like stuff and restoring Nah'ee to life.

Bruyah gasped. Eldest Great Dragon lifted her head and looked directly at Bruyah. Then she dipped her head down to nudge her baby. Nah'ee moved. A few more minutes and all the stone was gone. Nah'ee stood with her scales gleaming in every color possible and a few that aren't.

Nah'ee lifted her head. She looked at Eldest Great Dragon and gave a loud skreel. Eldest Great Dragon closed her wings around her Baby and hummed.

We waited.

And waited.

"Might as well get comfortable," Kembe said, sitting on a small rock. "Better have a couple of these," Kembe said, holding out a bag of Dragon beans.

"Thanks," I said. I took out a handful and offered one to Arald, then to Tahli. Finally, I held the bag out to Bruyah.

She took a bite out of one and frowned. She said something in that strange language Kisin had used. I looked at Tahli. The translator seemed to work for Spanish, but not that language. Grudgingly, Tahli nodded. Bruyah spoke again, "This is dragon food?"

"Dragon beans," Kembe answered. "Dragons eat much more than we do, but also less often," he explained. "I spend many hours waiting, so I keep these on hand." He offered one to Polter, who took one, but just held it in one claw.

Polter looked at Arald and me. *"Not too young,"* he said. *"Not flighty. Did job."*

"That's all right, Polter," I said. That was probably as close to an apology as we'd ever get from him. "You didn't know us." I nudged Arald. "Be nice," I told him silently.

He surprised me. *"Polter not in* any *world long time. Forgot."*

I nodded. I hadn't thought of that. Kembe and Polter had been gone over a hundred years looking to explore the Big Empty. "Kembe," I said, then cleared my throat. "Maybe this isn't the right time, but..."

"You wish to know what we found," Kembe said, munching on another Dragon bean. I nodded. "We found the Big Empty," he said. "But we got stuck when it grew suddenly. We didn't know how long we'd been stuck there until it was pushed away and we were able to return." Polter nodded.

"How did you get away from the Big Empty?" I asked.

"Something pushes the Big Empty even as it grows," he said slowly. "It cannot be seen. The Great Dragons are interested. They plan to go there. Polter and I are too old now. We will stay here in this world."

We sat and nibbled on Dragon beans. They don't all taste alike. I was lucky with the first few I ate. This time I tasted cabbage. The next one wasn't much better. Plain, unsweetened pumpkin.

I thought about Kembe having to stay in the Dragon World for the rest of his life. It isn't even a nice place to visit, really. Only rocks to sit on, log buckets to haul water in, and tough beans to eat. Polter found some bugs among the rocks, but I wouldn't want to eat those.

Just then, Tahli sat up straight. She flew to a tall rock nearby. Kembe stood and moved forward a bit. Polter went to his shoulder. "Eldest Great Dragon will speak to us now that her Baby sleeps," he said.

"Good dreams, I hope," I said. I got up from my rock and went to stand beside Kembe. Arald came to my shoulder. Bruyah edged behind us.

Eldest Great Dragon folded her wings back. Nah'ee lay curled in a ball between her feet. Eldest Great Dragon raised her head and turned to look at us. *"Pennamin and small ones do well."* She gave another of those toothy smiles. *"Bring my Child to me. To us,"* she said, pointing with one wing claw to the many dragons that now crowded the valley below us.

"Arald and Tahli and I had help, Eldest Great Dragon," I said, bowing low. "Oma and Kisin and his 'small one' named Yochi helped—and Bruyah did, too."

"Indeed," Eldest Great Dragon said, nodding. *"Those who kept the Nah'ee egg safe will be rewarded as well."*

Bruyah moved up beside me then. "Kisin and I did not know the Sacred Stone was an egg, but we kept it safe for many years, Eldest Great Dragon." Maybe she hadn't really changed. It seemed she wanted a reward, too.

Eldest Great Dragon stared at her a moment, then looked back at me. *"Pennamin come."*

Ben and Arald and The Lost Baby   Karel Henneberger

I gulped and walked closer until I was almost touching her feet. I look up—way up—until I could see her face. She lifted one wing claw and wiped at one eye. A drop of something—a tear, maybe—clung to the claw. Gently, she touched my head with the claw and I was soaking wet. All of me, not just my head. Water even dripped down into my shoes.

"Now Pennamin welcome in Dragon World. Always. None shall harm you."

I bowed as low as I could. "Thank you, Eldest Great Dragon. I am honored." Mom would be proud of how polite I could be.

"Pennamin. Small one name Arald. Come to Dragon World often. See Pru'ah, Nah'ee grow, learn. Be Nah'ee, Pru'ah friend."

I swallowed hard. Come back to the Dragon World often? Be a friend to Bruyah and the next Eldest One? I bowed even lower. "A great honor, Eldest Great Dragon," I said, though I wasn't too sure about that. Then, hesitantly, "Uh, how will I know when to come?"

"Pennamin, Arald will know," Taranoka growled. I sighed. Great. Another 'dragons decree' call.

Eldest Great Dragon called Bruyah to come forward. Another tear, another soaked human. She flicked a claw at Taranoka.

He spoke in his usual deep, rumbling voice, *"You are Pru'ah. You are Companion to Nah'ee. Gem'bah will teach,"* he said, pointing to Kembe. *"When time right, Pru'ah will return hooman world. When Nah'ee next Eldest One, dragon, hooman will know not always enemy."*

Bruyah bowed. Her eyes were wide. "We will learn together to live?" she asked, speaking slowly. Taranoka nodded. "The prophecy spoke truth, then." She grinned, bowed again, and stepped back.

"Bruyah was right all along," I thought to Arald.

"Part right," he answered. *"Not like us. Different. Not dragon-bound."*

Tahli chimed in, *"Not true partners. Maybe friends."*

Close enough, I thought to myself. Then I thought about what it might mean to be friends with an Eldest Great Dragon. Bruyah might have to stay here in the Dragon World for years. I shivered a bit. *"Maybe we could bring her something when we get the dragon call to come back,"* I thought.

Ben and Arald and The Lost Baby

Karel Henneberger

Arald looked at me with one eye. *"Maybe trade for Dragon beans."*

"Maybe," I said. "Mom would like some of them, I know."

Arose and Chobah appeared. Taranoka waved a wing claw at us to go. One large foot claw moved to keep Bruyah from coming with us. Once we were aboard our dragon transports, I looked down at her. She was standing proudly near Eldest Great Dragon, but her face didn't look proud. She looked more than a bit scared.

How would Kisin know what had happened, I wondered. Bruyah had been chosen to be the next Mamos, but it would be years before she could go home. "Maybe we could go through to the Black Line Rock and tell him," I said silently to Arald.

In my head, I heard the Eldest Great Dragon say in a strangely soft voice, *"Link gone. Man will know."* I swallowed hard. Arald's claws tightened. He had heard her, too. Tahli chittered and nodded.

Chapter Twenty-Six—Home Again

At the portal ledge, I looked down at the crowd of dragons there. They looked back at us. They didn't look ominous this time, even without Kembe or Polter. No teeth. No smoke. "We're always welcome now," I thought to Arald, remembering the Eldest Great Dragon's words. "It would probably be polite to say goodbye," I added, bowing.

Tahli chittered and dipped her head. Arald tilted his head, then leaned way forward, trying to bow the way I did. I caught him just in time. "Dragons can't bow that way," I told him. "Just do what Tahli did."

Many of the dragons below nodded back.

We turned and I leaned against the zigzag mark on the cliff. Seconds later, I barely caught my balance before Dad grabbed me in a big hug. Arald let out a small skreel and hopped onto Dad's shoulder, then flew down to grab a bacon sandwich Oma held out.

"Ouch! I see why all your shirts have padded shoulders," Dad said rubbing his own unpadded shoulder. He waved toward the blanket.

"Where's the girl?" Dad asked looking past me.

"She's to stay in the Dragon World and learn with Nah-ee," I answered. "I don't envy her," I added.

"You didn't take long," Oma said, handing me a sandwich and cup of juice.

I looked around. It had been full dark when we had entered the portal. It was still full dark. "We were there a long time," I said, frowning.

"Dragon World time different," Tahli said, then crunched down on her favorite nutcake.

Oma nodded. "Apparently, time doesn't move in the same way here and there. What was long for you was only a couple of hours here. Bracken brought blankets and food."

"And," Dad said, smiling, "a note from Mom. She made the bacon sandwiches."

"Mom's here? At Oma's?" I grinned.

Arald said, *"Mom make good bacon. Pancakes? Honey?"* he added.

"Well, now that you know Mom knows all about dragons and Oma, we thought it would be all right," Dad said with a glance at Oma. He looked at Arald. "Maybe pancakes for breakfast."

"I always knew Benjamin would do well," Oma said giving Dad the look that always made me start thinking about what I might have done wrong.

"Yes. Well, I was going to tell him last year, but..." Dad mumbled.

"But the Big Empty intruded," I finished.

"Yes," Oma nodded. "Things did get a bit exciting for a while."

"How about we get back to the house and you can tell us all about your time in the Dragon World," Dad suggested.

I was tired. I thought back, trying to put everything in some kind of order in my head. It had still been dark when we got up in Colombia. And it had already been dark again before we went through the portal. Then there was the time spent in the Dragon World and...

I didn't remember falling asleep, but I woke up just as we were climbing the last section of the cliff to Oma's house. I was lying on Bracken, my feet hanging down on each side. My hands were caught in his mane. Dad was walking beside us with one arm around me.

"Hungry," Arald said sleepily from my pack.

I jerked upright. "Wow. I really *was* tired," I said to Dad.

"You fell asleep with a mouth full of sandwich," Dad said with a smile. He helped me down from Bracken's back. "Luckily, Bracken and Gorse hadn't gone far." He paused. "Well," he said slowly, *"maybe* it was luck."

"Hello, down there!" That was Mom. She was standing on the porch that overlooked the Valley. "I have some soup and pie if you're hungry."

Now that I was awake, I realized I was as hungry as Arald. I thanked Bracken for the ride. He nodded and he and Gorse headed on past Oma's house and, probably, down to that farmer's barn.

Mom had made more bacon, too. Arald gobbled at least seven pieces. Tahli calmly ate one of the buttered rolls Mom had laid out on the table. I was scooping the last cherry from my second piece of Mom's fresh cherry pie, when I noticed everyone looking at me. "Huh?" I said, raising one eyebrow.

"Just waiting for you to finish eating so you can tell us about your adventure," Mom said. She handed Arald a small piece of bacon that had dropped on the table.

"Oh. Well, Oma knows all the early parts. Did you know, Dad, that she speaks Spanish?" I asked. He just nodded and moved his hand in a circle—keep talking.

I drew in a big breath. Where to start? *"Tell fun car part,"* Arald suggested.

I shook my head. He had enjoyed that trip a lot more than I had. "Well," I said. I stood up and began to pace the way Bruyah had when she told the story of the First Mother and the Sacred Stone. I drew in another breath, let it out, and began.

I told about the Kocqui and the Sacred Stone. And how Nah'ee meant 'dreams truth' or something like that, so when she was scared, everyone felt her fear. Hmmm. Pacing really does help you remember stuff, I thought.

Ben and Arald and The Lost Baby Karel Henneberger

"Well, done, Benjamin," Oma said. "The Mamos is also dragon-bound." She turned to Dad. "The First Mother ceremony was interesting, James. The symbols he used are found in many countries. The Sea is called the First Mother, but her symbol is a spider."

"Hmmm." Dad rubbed his chin. "Have to look into that. A lot of those so-called myths have a scientific basis, you know."

"Like the Big Empty," I said. "That was real, too. Kembe said dragons are interested in the Big Empty." I sat down again and licked one finger, then mopped up some pie crumbs from my dish. "Kembe's too old to go along with the dragons, Dad. He has to spend the rest of his life in the Dragon World," I said with a shiver.

Oma stood up. "It has been a very long time since the Old Man was in this world. I don't think he would like it any more than Polter did. Now," she added, "James, you and Ann will sleep in your old bed. Benjamin, you will take the cot in the corner."

I blinked. Cot? In the corner? I looked around the room. Sure enough, there was a cot in the corner by the door. Of course. It was needed.

I had a sudden thought. Jeanie. She was supposed to be home by now. "How did you explain this trip to Jeannie?" I asked Dad.

"Oh. Grandma Andrews wanted Jeannie to see a real stage play, but they could only get tickets for tomorrow night. So we'll be home before they are," he explained with a grin. "Convenient, no?"

I grinned back. "Convenient, yes. Dragons do get their way, don't they?"

Mom ruffled my hair. I hate that. She gave me a hug and kissed my forehead. That I like. "What dragons decree, you know…"

"…shall certainly be," Dad, Oma, and I said together.

"Pancakes with honey?" Arald chimed in hopefully.

Everyone, even Tahli laughed at that. "Pancakes with honey for breakfast," Mom promised with a giggle.

For another Ben and Arald adventure see:

Ben and Arald and the Big Empty.

www.ingramcontent.com/pod-product-compliance
Lightning Source LLC
Chambersburg PA
CBHW050737250626
47155CB00005B/1809